To the seekers
Believe in your dreams

To Candyne.

Enjoy.

Eileen Rolland.

Other books by Eileen Rolland

The Chrysalis Trilogy:
Friends in High Places
The Chrysalis Effect
Travelling Light

www.eileenrolland.com

ISLE OF SOMEWHERE

Eileen Rolland

Published in 2021 by Eileen Rolland

Publishing services by Lumphanan Press
www.lumphananpress.co.uk

Printed by Imprint Digital, UK

ISBN: 978-1-9168797-0-6

Sometimes

In
all
the
rush
and
hurry
of
our
lives
we
need
so
much
just
now
and
then
to
find
an
island

I am grateful to Kenneth Steven for his kind permission to use this poem, which can be found in his book *Island, Collected Poems.* **kennethsteven.co.uk**

– Chapter 1 –

Mon 7 Sept 2009

I had that dream again last night, exactly the same as last time, well, almost. I'm walking through this little village, nothing special, just a few houses and shops. The road winds round to the left and leads up a steep hill. As I climb the hill, I see a small waterfall on the right and somehow, I know I have to walk through it, or behind it really, to the other side. I walk up to the waterfall. It's not very big, twice my height and almost the same across. Despite being small, it's quite rapid and I worry, not only about getting wet but also about being pounded by the force of the water. The water falls into a pool then out through a small stream. I walk up along the side of the stream and stand next to the falls. I notice that there's a gap at the side, a bit where the water at the edge is diverted slightly by the shape of the rocks on top. I can walk through into a small cave. There are steps there too, on the far side and towards the back. A natural configuration of the cave or stones placed there centuries ago and worn down over time, I can't tell. I climb them regardless. They lead to an opening at the top of the falls where the land is flat and coloured with grass and wildflowers. Stones line either side of the narrow river that feeds into the falls. There's something new this time. A short distance away is a wooden pier where a boat waits for me. That's when I woke up.

Ros leaned back against her pillows. Although she dreamed often, she seldom remembered detail, so the dreams disappeared when she woke and were easily forgotten. This dream was different. Not only was it particularly vivid, but this was the second time she'd had it in the past two months. Why would she have the same dream twice if it didn't mean anything? She closed her eyes and thought about the different images she'd seen – the village, the hill, the waterfall and now the boat. Why a boat? It must mean something. She read through what she'd written but could think of nothing else to add so she put down her pen and returned her diary to the top drawer of her bedside table. Maybe she would have the dream again and maybe there would be more detail, more clarity. Meanwhile, she had to get ready. Monday was a workday. She thought about her mum and wondered how she was feeling today. Perhaps she would get the chance to call her later.

Most people think a library is a quiet place to work. That's not always the way Ros found it. Certainly, the reading rooms were quiet and even General Lending and Reference, but she worked at Reception in the main hall. That was usually busy. People were constantly coming and going, plus her desk was right across from the Children's area, which was open-plan and could be hectic at times. There were days when she could barely hear herself think. She wasn't complaining though. Ros liked her work and got on well with most of the staff. Besides, it was only three days a week.

"We can give you more hours, if you want," Eleanor said. "You know Kath's leaving."

Ros was fond of her supervisor. "Yes, I had heard, but I'm happy with the hours I have. I appreciate the offer though."

Eleanor drew closer and lowered her voice. "It's not common

knowledge, but," she glanced around to make sure no one was listening, "I'm leaving too."

Ros' breath stopped dead in her throat. Her eyes widened and she felt her heart sink. Thoughts flooded her mind. Eleanor had been the one who had welcomed her on her first day. She had put her at ease right from the start. She had explained procedures and answered all her questions. She had introduced her to the other members of staff. She and Eleanor had become more than just co-workers. Ros respected her and they worked well together. Each was willing to help the other if an unexpected problem arose. Now that friendship, that support, was being ripped away from her.

"You can't leave, Eleanor. You just can't."

"If I don't leave now they might have to carry me out. I should have retired a year ago; now's the time." Eleanor's expression was one of resolve tinged with sadness. "Don't say anything, will you. It's not official yet. There are still some things to sort out."

"No. I won't say anything because you're not going. We won't let you." Ros rummaged around for reasons, solid reasons, something Eleanor couldn't argue with, but she found none. "You're not old enough," she fumbled, "and, we would miss you. You're the one who holds everything together. You keep us all right."

"Ahh, thank you, Ros, that's really nice but I'm older than you think and I'm ready to take a back seat, do something different with my life. Besides, I know you will manage fine without me, everyone will. I've seen how you all work, don't forget."

Ros sighed. "What will you do? Do you have any plans?"

"Not yet. It would just be nice to have some time to myself, catch my breath and see what life brings my way."

"We really will miss you, you know that. Any idea of when you'll leave?"

"Probably in the next month or two. There's paperwork to sort out and they have to advertise the post to find a replacement."

Ros hadn't thought that far ahead. "Will it be internal?" There were a few people she knew who would love the supervisor's job, and a few that she would rather not have as her boss.

"It might be to start with. If they don't get anyone, they'll most likely open it to the public. Why? Are you interested?"

"Oh, no thank you. You make the job look easy but I know you have had some real trials and taken a lot of flak from the directors, and members of the public. Anyway, it doesn't really matter who gets in. I wish you well, I really do. You've done a great job here and you should enjoy your retirement."

"Thanks Ros." Before turning to leave, Eleanor looked at Ros and put her index finger to her lips.

Ros understood, and nodded her compliance.

The conversation with Eleanor had upset Ros, although she couldn't help feeling pleased at the thought of Eleanor having told her first. She began to think of her own position. Her job was interesting without being overly challenging. Eleanor had a way of working with people without being authoritarian or demanding. They all worked together as a team, each one knowing his or her role and how those roles fitted together.

Ros' remit included talking to people, directing them to the section they were looking for and answering any questions they had. She liked that best. There were other things too. The library had information about short courses at the college, for example, as well as talks and workshops being held at various places by various people. Members of the public often came in and asked about volunteering opportunities, drawn, no doubt, by the posters that lined the notice boards on the walls. The library stocked leaflets from a host of local organisations and community groups, and Ros had been successful in helping people find something rewarding to do with their spare time. There was something particularly satisfying about that.

The variety of placements available had astounded her when she had first started working there. Most people couldn't make up their minds. They asked about this group and that, asked questions that Ros couldn't answer and invariably went away with a handful of leaflets to consider in their own time. Suzanne had been different. She had been one of the easy ones. As soon as she heard about the library's Archives, she knew that was what she wanted to do. Ros had been surprised at the speed of Suzanne's decision and having already pulled out a few more leaflets for consideration, found that she had to put them all back again.

"That was quick," she had chuckled. "Did you know that was what you wanted to do?"

"Not really," Suzanne had replied. "I heard the word 'archives' and something clicked. I just know it's right for me."

Immediately, Ros was intrigued. How did she 'just know'? She hadn't taken any time to consider all the aspects of the work. She hadn't asked any questions. She didn't know what hours might be required or what type of work would be expected. How could she possibly 'just know' it was right for her? Still, there was no denying that Suzanne had been happy with her decision. She had agreed on the spot to come in two mornings a week. As it happened, the two days she had chosen were two of the days that Ros was at work. Inevitably they saw each other on those days and chatted easily, mainly about the weather to begin with. In the four months since Suzanne had started volunteering, she and Ros had become good friends and often met up for coffee or sometimes lunch. Ros admired her. She seemed to have an air of wisdom about her, not superiority though. Suzanne was very down-to-earth and had a great deal of respect for other people as well as an understanding, or at least an empathy, with their problems. She seemed to be able to get right to the heart of the matter in any discussion.

An incident came to mind. Ros recalled a time when they had gone to a garden centre and went into the cafe for coffee and cake. Suzanne had offered to pay but Ros had jumped in and refused to let her, insisting that she pay instead. Suzanne graciously accepted but later that day they had a discussion about giving and receiving. Suzanne had gently said to Ros that she was very good at giving but perhaps less good at receiving. Ros considered her words later and felt ashamed. She realised her insistence on paying had embarrassed Suzanne, or worse, it had even prevented her from having the opportunity to give. She hadn't meant to upset her friend. Why had she felt so strongly about it? Why had she been so pushy? She could simply have offered to pay next time, they met up often enough. It was only after thinking about all this for some time that Ros realised it wasn't about the coffee at all. It was about her attitude generally. It was about giving and receiving, well, anything really. It was about knowing when to give and when to receive; when to ask for help and when to offer it. She thought about people she knew who wouldn't accept help when they needed it or felt they had to be strong in the face of overwhelming difficulty. Was she like that?

She had learned a lot that day. She realised too, that Suzanne had handled the situation very delicately – just enough to make her point and get Ros to think out the details for herself. She admired the skill with which Suzanne had put her point across. Since then, Ros decided to be more open-minded generally and certainly more open to receiving help when she needed it, but why was this all coming back to her now? Then a thought occurred to her, a wonderful, curious thought. She wondered now if Suzanne was any good at interpreting dreams.

– Chapter 2 –

Mondays were usually quiet days and this one was no exception, at least on the outside. But between trying to understand the dream, concern for her mum and the shock of Eleanor's news, Ros had a lot on her mind. She needed to clear her head. 'Best to keep busy,' she thought and began by taking down out-of-date posters and putting up the new ones that had arrived that morning by internal mail. This job was never-ending, but they had to be checked every day or two to keep the information current. She'd been embarrassed before when people asked about events that were no longer available.

This task was just part of the routine and Ros didn't have to give it much thought but today, for some reason, a few of the notices caught her attention. A local organisation was running a First Aid training course. That would be interesting. First aid was something everyone should know. She made a mental note of the date and time. There was also notification of an 'Evening of Mediumship' at one of the branch libraries. Ros wasn't sure if she believed in that but her recent pledge to be more open-minded made her at least consider it. She considered it for all of two minutes before dismissing the idea, convincing herself that she probably wouldn't have time anyway. Although her evenings were usually free, it was the only excuse she could think of.

She tidied her desk, caught up with some work left over

from the weekend and found herself with time on her hands. Catching a glimpse of Kath struggling to put books back on the upper shelves, she offered to help.

"When's the baby due?" Ros asked.

Kath was trying to put one of the bigger books on a higher shelf but found it difficult to reach and didn't want to climb on the little step ladder. Ros reached out her hand and gratefully, Kath gave the book to her.

"Another month to go," Kath said. "If I get much bigger, I won't be able to move at all."

"You shouldn't be stretching," Ros said, stepping onto the ladder and reaching up to put the book in its place.

"I know."

"Can you keep an eye on my desk? I'll take care of these."

"Oh, cheers, Ros. You want a coffee?"

"Yeah, that would be nice, ta."

Ros pulled the wooden trolley through the aisles of books that filled the General Lending section and began putting each book back in place. Kath had been very well organised, arranging the books according to their reference code, so it was easy to work through them all and the job didn't take long.

There were plenty of books for Crime Fiction. These, along with Romance, took up the bulk of those on the trolley. The Health and Well-being section only had a few and Ros worked quickly. When she picked up one book, however, she stopped. She could easily have overlooked it. It was just another book, but somehow her attention was drawn to it. She stood with it in her right hand and found herself unable to put it down. She looked at the title, and then looked again. 'Lucid Dreaming'. She had heard the term before but didn't really know what it meant so turned the book over to read the blurb on the back. She didn't understand half of the description given but she got the gist. The idea of being aware that you were dreaming and actually being able to influence aspects of the dream seemed bizarre, intriguing certainly but totally bizarre nonetheless.

Bringing her attention back to the task at hand, she placed that book on the shelf then, putting the last few away, went to join Kath at the reception desk. They shared coffee and conversation. Kath was pleasant company and, in Ros' opinion, would be a good mother.

"Do you know what you're having?" Ros asked.

"A girl," Kath beamed.

"Scans are great these days, aren't they? They can tell you so much."

"Oh, they didn't tell me at the hospital. They could have, of course, but I didn't want them to."

Ros was confused. "So, how do you know it's a girl then?"

Kath looked a little sheepish. "People laugh when I tell them but," she paused to watch Ros' face as she spoke, "I saw her."

"You 'saw' her?" Ros was even more confused.

"Yes, in my mind. She's so beautiful, brown eyes and loads of dark, curly hair. I know it sounds weird, but I was relaxing one night, just watching TV and feeling a bit drowsy. I closed my eyes and this image came into my mind and I knew it was my baby. I just knew."

Ros could only smile. She didn't know what to say. Here was someone else who 'just knew' something and had no explanation other than that. When she thought about it, the Archives had certainly been the right choice for Suzanne. Maybe Kath was right about her baby too, but how did that all work? Kath saw Ros' puzzled expression and understood it immediately.

She smiled back at Ros and finishing her coffee said, "I guess we'll know in a few weeks whether I'm right or not."

A practical answer Ros thought, but not an explanation. "Oh, I'm sure you are," she said. It sounded feeble. Then she added, "I wish I could feel things like that."

"Maybe you have to have a baby," Kath said and they both laughed.

The rest of the day went slowly. Ros was bored and a bit unsettled but, on the up-side, she had time to think. Why had the book on lucid dreaming caught her attention so much? Maybe she was meant to read it. That thought surprised her. She straightened her back and told herself not to be ridiculous, but she couldn't shake the feeling that something was going on, something she couldn't make sense of. It was as if she was being nudged. That was the only way she could explain it.

She gave a little laugh at how fanciful she was becoming and tried to get back to her work but all these thoughts gave her an idea. She knew the section on health and well-being wasn't very big. There was only a handful of books and most of those where on alternative medicines. She wondered if there would be anything on dreams and their meanings. At her break she went to have a look.

The computer showed that there were two books on that subject and one, The Psychology of Dreaming, looked a bit obscure, technical and not what she was looking for. The only book the library had that she thought might be helpful was out on loan and wasn't due back in for two weeks. She wished Suzanne was there. Ros always found her easy to talk to. They talked about loads of things and their conversations were always thought-provoking, even insightful. She knew she could ask Suzanne anything without worrying about being criticised or judged. She would be in tomorrow. Maybe they could talk then. Ros would be working but her lunch break was about the same time that Suzanne finished in the Archives. She would catch her at ten o'clock, as she came in, and arrange to meet for lunch. Hopefully, she wouldn't have any prior arrangements. Besides, Ros suddenly remembered, it was her turn to pay.

That night, Ros had the dream again.

– Chapter 3 –

"Ooh, dreams," Suzanne cooed. "I love dreams. I'm not sure about interpreting them but I find them fascinating." Suzanne had a sudden thought and her face took on a worried expression. "You're not having bad dreams, are you?"

"No, just recurring ones."

Suzanne's eyes widened. She leaned forward and rested her chin on her hand. "That's interesting. Are they romantic? Are you naked?"

"No! Why would you even ask that?"

"Could be important. Do you feel vulnerable?"

"No, not really."

"How do you feel?"

"I don't know," Ros said, a bit flustered. "If anything, I suppose I feel a little unsettled at the moment."

"How long has it been since you and Matthew split up?" Suzanne opened a sachet of brown sugar and stirred it into her cappuccino.

"About a year and a half, maybe closer to two years, actually. Why?"

"Do you think it might have something to do with that?" Suzanne asked, still stirring.

Ros hadn't thought of that, but she took a moment to consider it now. "No," she said at last. "I can't see how. I love being alone. My time and my space are my own. I make my own decisions. I spend my own money. No. Leaving Matthew was one of the best decisions I ever made. I just feel like something's missing, like I'm meant to be doing something else but I don't know what it is."

"And you think the dream has something to do with it?" Suzanne repeated, taking a bite of her brie and cranberry toastie.

"I don't know," Ros moaned. "That's the whole point. I've had it three times now and I can't get it out of my mind, so I'm thinking there must be some reason for it. Maybe my brain is trying to tell me something but it's so cryptic I can't figure it out."

Ros pushed some of the salad around on her plate with a fork. Suzanne was sympathetic.

"Some say dreams are a way of sorting out the information you've received that day," she offered. "You know, categorising things and making associations. Some say it's the subconscious working out problems. Still others say you're channelling information from outwith your 'self' to help you progress along your life's path. It depends who you ask."

"What do you think?"

"Who knows? Maybe all of them. Maybe we get different kinds of dreams for different reasons. Anyway, tell me what you remember of your dream and we'll see if we can put some ideas together."

Ros related as much of the dream as she could, in as much detail as she could. In telling it, other factors came to mind; the lack of colour, for instance, as she walked through the village and the fact that there were no people about. She gave an accurate description of the waterfall and realised that it was only when she reached the top of the falls that she saw colour in the dream, in the grass and flowers that lined the riverbank, and the blue of the sky.

"And there's a pier and a boat waiting for you?" Suzanne asked.

"Yes."

"You don't go on the boat?"

"No."

"Well, from the little I know about dream symbols," Suzanne paused, gathering her thoughts, "I believe that modes of transport – cars, buses, trains, and so on – represent your journey through life."

"So that would be the boat," Ros offered.

Suzanne gave a little shrug. "It would seem reasonable, but you don't go on board so maybe something is stopping you."

"Like what?"

"Fear, probably. Maybe you're afraid of where the boat will take you. Maybe you're afraid of where life will take you."

Ros felt the impact of Suzanne's words. Was she really so afraid? It seemed a logical explanation, when she thought about it. "But I'm not aware of feeling afraid when I see the boat."

"What do you feel?"

"Nothing, really." Ros shrugged and took another moment to think. "I'm just surprised to see it, I guess."

"Nothing else?"

This was taxing Ros' brain. She closed her eyes and went over the scene in her mind. "It's a very nice looking boat," she acknowledged, "quite attractive really. And I want to go onto it but I seem to think it's not..." She stopped talking as the words she was about to say hit home. She looked at Suzanne who stared at her, entreating her to finish. Ros' voice was small. "It's as if I don't believe I deserve to go on board, as if it must be for someone else." Tears began to fill her eyes and she dabbed them with her napkin then blinked hard to stop their flow.

Suzanne's voice was soft, gentle. "Is there anyone else around?"

"No."

"Whose dream is it?"

"Mine," Ros said, taking a deep breath. "It's my dream."

"And who is the boat waiting for?" Suzanne gave her friend a little smile. Ros felt the power of it and straightened her back.

"Me. The boat is waiting for me."

"Well then, when you have the dream again, go on board."

"So you think I will have the dream again?"

Suzanne nodded. "Until you figure out what it's all about, I suspect you will."

Ros sighed and considered all that Suzanne had told her, taking time to go over the different aspects in her mind. Then something occurred to her. "Wait. What do you mean, when I have the dream again, go on board? How do I do that if I'm dreaming?"

"Tell yourself you want to go onto the boat. Say it to yourself before you go to sleep: 'If I have the dream again tonight, I want to go on the boat.' It's as simple as that."

"It can't be that simple."

"Try it."

Ros was amazed. She thought of the book on lucid dreaming as she looked at her friend and smiled. "You scare me sometimes."

"I scare myself sometimes. Anyway, come on, finish your coffee. We have some shopping to do before you go back to work."

Obediently, Ros finished her latte, paid the bill and followed Suzanne up the busy High Street, curious to know what she had in mind. They came to a stationery shop and Ros followed her inside. They browsed books and magazines; pens and pencils;

folders, files and wrapping papers. When they got to the notebooks, they stopped. Suzanne didn't take long to choose one. It was A5 size and had a pleasant depiction of a street cafe with a bistro style table and two chairs. There was a tree off to one side and an awning over the door of the cafe on the other. It was all decorated in soft pastel colours, mostly pinks and greens.

"That's lovely," Ros said. "You got some writing to do?"

"It's not for me," Suzanne smiled. "I'm glad you like it."

Before Ros could respond, Suzanne was heading toward the cashier. She stopped on the way to pick up a pen the colour of which co-ordinated perfectly with the notebook. She paid for her purchases and handed the bag to Ros.

"It's only for dreams, okay?"

"I have a diary," Ros said, still a bit bewildered.

"It's not a diary, it's a journal, a dream journal. It's special, only for dreams, and maybe meditations if you do that too."

"I don't really."

"Daydreams, then. Maybe meditation will come later. It's just helpful if you have a separate book to record these things, a book you like and will enjoy writing in."

"Do you do meditation?" Ros wanted to know.

"I took a course once. It's just another tool you can use. Some people find it easy, others don't. Don't worry about it just now. Focus on your dreams."

"I don't always remember my dreams. They seem to disappear as soon as I wake up."

"Not this one, though."

"No."

"Just write what you do remember. Don't stress about it. Sometimes when you read it over again, even days later, something else comes to mind."

Ros wanted to ask Suzanne more about meditation. In fact, loads of questions were coming to mind, but there was no time. Ros had to get back to work and Suzanne was on her way home.

The afternoon went quickly. There was a school party in for a story-telling session and Ros helped Karen, the senior worker in the Children's section, to get the props ready beforehand. Ros had as little contact with Karen as possible. She could be abrupt and say things in a way that upset and hurt people yet often seemed oblivious to the upset she'd caused. Ros was more interested in making sure the children would have a good experience of the library, so she also helped set up tables and chairs for a colouring competition and juice afterwards before they left.

There had only been twenty-two children, but it had felt like a hundred and twenty-two. They seemed to be everywhere at once. They weren't badly behaved, just curious and excited. There was a lot of clearing up to do later on. Crayons littered the floor. Books had been taken off the shelves and left strewn around the soft seating area or placed, back to front or upside down, back on the shelves, although not in their proper places. By the time all that had been done, it was almost time to go home. Ros tidied her desk. She liked to leave everything neat and in place for the next day when Jennifer would be in. She picked up her notebook and pen and placed them next to her coat and handbag, but there was something she had to do before she left. She went around to the General Lending section and checked out the book on lucid dreaming.

– Chapter 4 –

The flat Ros lived in wasn't very big, but it was hers and she liked it to look nice. She often used her days off not only to catch up with her cleaning but also to do some of those odd little jobs that cropped up from time to time. This was how she had spent most of her morning and, with the bulk of the housework done, she rewarded herself with a coffee and a chocolate biscuit. She sat down at the small, round, kitchen table and looked out the window. The book on Lucid Dreaming sat where she had placed it the night before, on the worktop next to the fridge-freezer. She looked at it, uncertain now of any benefit it might have. 'Probably nonsense,' she thought, turning back to her coffee. 'It's only a dream, for crying out loud. Why am I letting it get me in a tangle?' She looked back at the book and, recognising the fact that she had felt strongly enough at the time to bring it home, she might as well see what it had to say. She went over to the worktop, lifted the book and began to read. She found it surprisingly well written and easy to follow, with clear explanations and helpful diagrams. 'So far, so good,' she thought. There were exercises too, techniques and practises designed to help the reader 'obtain lucidity'. The first one was described in detail and sounded easy enough. She would try it later, maybe tonight when she would be more restful and have less on her mind.

The washing machine whirred noisily in the background,

bringing Ros back to her chores. She closed the book, finished her coffee and turned her attention to her to do list. She looked at the clock. If she could get as much as possible done today, it would free up time tomorrow when she would be with her mum. She realised some things would have to wait till another time and quickly read through the list to see what could be put off. She didn't believe in overworking. Her part-time job suited her well, in terms of striking a balance between work and leisure time. She had seen too many people work themselves into the ground, her father, for example, and she was determined she wasn't going to let that happen to her. Life was too short and money wasn't everything.

She looked around and sighed. 'Well,' she said out loud, wrapping her apron around her waist and tying the strings at the back, 'if I don't start, I'll never finish.' She did as much as she could by mid-afternoon and found she was running out of steam. There was still an hour or so before she would have to get dinner ready. The book beckoned and would no longer be ignored. She sighed as she lifted it and, taking it into the sitting room, curled into her comfy, reclining armchair, put her feet up on the matching footrest and began to read. She read the first chapter over again, taking in as much detail as possible. If she was going to do this, she might as well do it properly. She wanted to absorb what was being said, not just skim through. She also wanted to be able to do the exercises without stopping to check she hadn't forgotten something.

From the little she knew, it seemed to her that the first exercise was the basis of meditation. She had time to try it now, a practice session in preparation for the real thing later in the evening. She followed the instructions to sit comfortably, close her eyes, become aware of her body and focus on her breathing. Those were all physical things. She could do those all right, but what was difficult was 'calming the chatter' in her head. She hadn't realised so much chatter was there in the first place. Random thoughts interrupted her and her mind wandered. She started over again but was disappointed when the same thing happened. She decided that it would be better to wait until she was going to bed. She would be tired and more likely to be able to relax. She put the book down and leaned back into the chair. She was just about to close her eyes when the phone rang.

"Hello? Ros? Is that you, Ros? Are you there?"

"Hello, Mum. Yes, yes, it's me. Are you all right?"

"Yes, I'm fine. I was just wondering if you were coming over tomorrow."

"Mum, I come and see you every Thursday. You know that."

"Don't be angry with me. I just wanted to make sure."

"I'm not angry with you, Mum. Don't get upset. I'll be over tomorrow, as usual. We can go out and get some shopping. Maybe we could go to that little tea room you like and have lunch. Would you like that?"

There was a pause. "Yes. That would be lovely. I just wanted to make sure. You understand, don't you?"

"Yes Mum, I understand. It's okay."

"Okay. Thank you. I'll see you tomorrow then. Bye."

Ros said good-bye to the dialling tone. Her mother had always been a bit forgetful but now she seemed nervous and confused. Was her condition worsening? The doctor had said that would happen. Ros had hoped he was wrong. These things played on her mind and she began to wonder how her mother was coping on her own. Ros was sure she was fine; she just had an off day from time to time. But if things were getting worse for her, the time might come when she needed some extra help. This thought gathered momentum and Ros found herself thinking ahead. She wondered, ultimately, if her mum would even be able to stay in her own home, the house she had lived in all her married life. That would be a big upheaval.

Someone at work had mentioned care homes months ago, and suggested Ros give it some thought, saying that although it wasn't something that was needed immediately, there was no harm in being prepared. Ros had dismissed the idea at the time. Her mother had seemed to recover well after her mini-stroke. It was true she'd had a few falls since then but Ros had taken her to the doctor and got her checked over. There was never any real problem. She had always been able to see to her mother's needs. But now it occurred to her that if those needs were changing, she would have to change too. There was never any question that she would take care of her mother as she got older. They had always been there for each other. But she was still working. What if Mum needed more help than Ros could give her? Perhaps it would be an idea to make some preliminary enquiries, just to find out. The thought saddened her and she sighed. They weren't at that stage yet and Ros knew her mother wouldn't like it. Although gentle natured, she had always been an independent woman, especially since Dad died. Maybe there would be an opportunity tomorrow to raise the subject or even just to introduce the idea to her mother, see her reaction, determine what she wanted and let her have some time to think about it. Ros knew she would have to be tactful.

By the time evening came Ros was tired, physically and mentally. She had a hot bath using her favourite bath oil and took some time to soak, letting the heat soften the muscles in her back and legs. She was feeling quite mellow as she got into bed. She propped the pillows up behind her and, picking up the book, read through the exercise once more. Then she snuggled down, warm and comfortable, into her bed, closed her eyes and focused on the weight of her body against the mattress, her head on the pillow. She became aware of her breathing and felt it slowing down as she relaxed more and more into the exercise. She had a slight sensation of floating, a feeling she had never experienced before. She decided she liked it. With every breath, she drifted further toward sleep and just before sleep engulfed her completely, she whispered, "If I have that dream again tonight, I want to go on the boat... I want to go on the boat."

– Chapter 5 –

Ros walked through the village, as usual, on the far side of the street. Across the road on her right was a row of neat houses. They were quite close to each other and all looked exactly the same. Each had two storeys and there were no front gardens. The door to each house was only a step or two off the pavement. They were all grey and uninteresting.

She couldn't tell what was on her left side. The whole area was shrouded in mist. When she looked down, she saw that she was walking on a concrete pavement, the same as the one that ran in front of the houses on the other side of the road. Next to the pavement there was a low wooden barrier – short wooden struts with a longer piece of wood joining each of them across the top. The whole thing came to just below her knees. Beyond the barrier was the fog. She was curious as to what might actually be there – perhaps a park, a small lake or even a sheer drop. She kept walking. It seemed more important to get to where she was going than to pay attention to her surroundings.

The road curved round to the left and began to get steeper. She continued walking. She knew she was coming up to the waterfall. Just before she reached it, she looked across the road and saw an old house. That one hadn't been there before. She would have remembered it. This house was different from the rest, similar in size and shape but, being on a slope, it had a few more steps up to the door, and it was more colourful. It was made of red brick with a green roof and the door was painted a deep blue. There were tiny coloured lights all around the window frame. Intrigued, she went over to see what was inside.

The window was high up and, even standing on her toes, she couldn't see very much. From what she could see, it looked as though the house was being used as a shop. She opened the door and went in. The house looked much bigger inside than she had thought it would. There were shelves and cupboards, cabinets and counters with all kinds of things on display. One counter had fabric with needles, threads and a variety of sewing notions, knitting needles and wool. Another had kitchen utensils, cake tins, cookie cutters and mixing bowls. As she walked around she saw paints and brushes, papers and pencils, wire, string, cardboard, wood, nails, almost everything one could imagine. It occurred to her that these were all creative things – things that could be used to make whatever one needed to make.

"That's right," a voice said. It was a woman's voice, pleasantly soft and quite cheery.

Ros looked around to see a petite, middle-aged lady with hair the colour of sand, standing beside one of the counters.

"We have everything you'll ever need," she continued.

Ros was curious. "But how did you know…?

"The thing is," the lady interrupted, "most people don't know what they need. Oh, yes, they know they need something, they know that all right, but they have no idea what it is. So what do they do? They try to obtain everything they think it might be – clothes, furniture, cars, houses… sometimes even drugs. They're always disappointed. Always."

"Why am I here?" Ros asked.

"You came in. You must be looking for something. As I said,

we have everything you need. You might not know what it is yet but when you do, just ask for it. We do a great delivery service."

The woman smiled and the next thing Ros knew, she was outside again, continuing her walk up the hill. Although she felt a little confused and wanted to go back to the shop, it seemed more important, for now at least, to get where she knew she had to go. The waterfall was just a little further along. As usual, Ros went in behind the falls and walked up the stone steps in the cave. When she reached the top, she was on the riverbank and just a short distance in front of her was the little, wooden pier where the boat waited for her.

She walked slowly toward the boat. It was quite beautiful, a small paddle steamer with the great paddle wheel at the back. The boat was brightly coloured, mostly white but with blue and red decoration. She called out but there seemed to be no one about. The boat bobbed gently back and forth with the flow of the water. There was a gangplank that led from the edge of the pier onto the boat but a metal barrier prevented access. Frustrated she looked for another way to board but saw none. She thrust her hands in the pockets of her coat and turned to leave. To her surprise, she felt a piece of paper in her hand and drew it out to look at it. It was a ticket, a ticket to board the boat. She looked up at the boat again. The barrier was gone. She took a deep breath and walked along the pier, up the gangplank and onto the lower deck. There were square windows all along the port side. She tried to look in as she passed them, but couldn't see anything. Eventually she found a door and, opening it slowly, cautiously, she went inside.

To her amazement, the lounge area she had just entered was full of people. There were men and women, young and old, from all different backgrounds and cultures. Some sat in easy chairs talking or looking out the window. Some sat at tables with a variety of food and drink in front of them, some of which Ros had never seen before. Some looked at her as she walked by. Some smiled, others paid no attention. No one spoke to her. She looked around for a member of staff, someone who could tell her what was happening and what she was expected to do. She saw no one who would fit that description.

Over by the window was a seat that had a little table in front of it and, sitting down, she looked around at the scene before her. 'So many people', she thought. 'Who are they? Why were they all here?' When she looked back to her table she found a coffee had been placed there for her, a latte, just the way she liked it. She looked around again but saw no waiter or waitress. She decided to accept what was happening. Reaching out, she lifted her coffee and took a sip. That's when the boat began to sail.

The chair she was in was very comfortable and it was easy to relax. She leaned her head back against the headrest and closed her eyes. She could hear the gentle hum of the engine and the rhythmic splish-splash of the water as the wheel turned. It was like a heartbeat. She could also hear the soft murmur of people talking. Fragments of conversation and distant laughter caught her attention but did not divert it. The muscles in her back began to soften. Words floated in the air like soap bubbles. She felt as if she only had to reach up and burst a bubble to hear what it had to say. She loved this dreamy state she was in, not awake but not asleep either. She could hear people talking but it was all in the distance. Words and phrases drifted around her head, only a few reached her consciousness – a hodgepodge of unassembled conversations. She allowed them to enter. This jumbled soup of thoughts, words, songs and ideas spun round in her head:

> "The flow of energy is always life-ward."
> "Don't cut yourself off from the healing a loving embrace can bring."
> "Open your eyes and see. Your thoughts create your reality."
> "We're all in the same boat."
> "Showing humility empowers you."
> "Do you think she can hear us?"

On hearing that, Ros' eyes opened wide. The scene before her was the same. People talked and laughed and ate, paying no attention to any of the others and certainly not to her. Still, she felt unsettled. Leaving her seat she walked around, taking in her surroundings. Stairs led to an upper deck and she climbed them. A few people sat on bench-type seats and looked out the large windows that lined both sides and crossed the front of the observation room, giving a view of the water on three sides. Some people stood outside along the railings taking in the view and the fresh, clean air. Ros decided that was what she would do. She went outside and walked to the bow of the boat, feeling incredibly tranquil despite her uncertainties. This contradiction puzzled her a little. She took a deep breath and looked around. There was nothing but water for as far as she could see. Light danced off the swell. The air was clean and sweet. She saw dolphins break the surface of the water and swim alongside. She had never seen anything so beautiful. She had never felt so beautiful. She breathed deeply and slowly as if breathing in more than just air, as if breathing in pure joy.

As she looked out in front of her, she thought she could see something off in the distance – a tiny speck that appeared to get bigger as they travelled toward it. Then she realised it was an island, and they were heading straight for it.

– Chapter 6 –

Immediately on waking, Ros reached for her dream journal and pen. She wrote furiously, trying to get every detail down before the dream evaporated. She wrote page after page until there was nothing left. When she stopped, she rested back against her pillow, the pen still in her hand, and tried to think of anything she may have missed out. She could think of nothing. Satisfied, she sat up and added a personal note:

I remember being on the boat and seeing the island. The next thing I remember is getting off the boat at the pier and walking back down through the village again. I have no recollection of what happened on the island, or even if I went onto the island at all. It's so frustrating!

Ros sighed, closed the book and put it back in the drawer. She was in the habit of getting up at the same time every morning whether or not it was a work day. It gave her day some structure. She went through her usual morning routine then sat down with a cup of tea. It was better to be as relaxed as possible before going to see her mum. Not that her mother was difficult, Ros loved being with her but the concern she had for her could be intense at times and often left her feeling tired and anxious. She felt helpless to be able to do anything for her, other than practical things, and their visits sometimes left Ros feeling mentally and emotionally exhausted. Today, as always, she wanted to look forward to seeing her mum and spending time with her.

The drive wasn't a long one, only a few minutes if the traffic was good. Ros stepped out of her car and stood for a moment looking at the house. It was old and could do with some freshening up. The front door was in the centre with windows of equal size to either side, one for the sitting room and one for the main bedroom. The garden at the front was mostly lawn. Narrow flower beds lined the straight, paved path that led to the door. Dad had also built brick planters under the windows where flowers and small shrubs now grew. It all looked very neat. Ros smiled at the thought of her mother having been out to work in the garden. Although it was something she enjoyed, she wasn't good at it and Ros had thought of getting a gardener in to keep things tidy. There were a lot of happy memories associated with this house. It had been a good house as she was growing up but she now realised that it was quite big – bigger than her mum needed, really. Ros wondered if it was getting to be too much for her to look after on her own. It was familiar though, and maybe that was more important. She went inside and found her mother in remarkably good spirits.

"Hello, Sweetheart," she chirped as Ros walked in. Ros smiled as she gave her a hug. It was a warm and sincere embrace. "You look wonderful."

"Oh, thank you, Mum. Are you ready to go out? I thought we could go to the shopping centre for a while and have a look at some clothes, maybe get you a new cardigan or something."

"I don't need a new cardigan," her mother said abruptly.

Ros was getting used to these fluctuations in temperament. She had to change the focus. "Well, I could do with one for work. We'll have a look anyway and see what they've got."

Her mother smiled. "Yes, we'll see what they've got," she repeated. Lifting her coat, she allowed Ros to help her put it on, then walked towards the door. Ros had to grab the handbag from the chair and hand it to her. Outside, she watched as her mother locked the door, then checked it was locked, then checked it again. Finally, they were on their way.

The shopping trip was more successful than anticipated. Ros bought a cardigan and her mother got a new pair of boots, fleece-lined and waterproof, with a good tread for walking on wet or icy ground. Winter was coming. She also bought a handbag to go with the boots. Ros was sure she had a dozen handbags in the house but if it made her mother happy, she was delighted.

It was as they were leaving the shops and heading towards Rosie's Tea Rooms that Ros' mother met someone she knew.

"Millicent. Hello, lovely to see you."

Ros' mother took a moment to process what was happening. "Oh, hello," she said at last. "I wasn't expecting to see you."

Ros just stood smiling at the man, then her mother, then the man again.

"Oh, I'm so sorry. Roslyn, this is Mr Fielding. Mr Fielding, my daughter, Roslyn."

"Pleased to meet you, Mr Fielding," Ros said.

"Oh, call me Gregory, please. Only my bank manager calls me Mr Fielding and it makes me nervous."

Ros smiled politely, then watched as this man and her mother chatted. He seemed friendly enough. He wasn't very tall and, Ros guessed, was about the same age as her mother. He was well dressed and from the brief conversation, she gathered that Gregory was one of her mother's neighbours. After a few minutes they said good-bye and the two women continued their walk to the tea rooms.

Ros understood why her mother liked this cafe. From the outside, it looked like an old-fashioned sweet shop with a bay window set with square panes of glass. There was a display of children's toys in the window, wooden toys mostly – a rocking horse, a tricycle and a number of smaller items. There were pull-along animals, building blocks and jigsaw puzzles, along with other things, a hula hoop, skates, jacks and marbles. Ros remembered playing with toys like those when she was very young. They were not like many of the modern toys that all seemed to need batteries or require charging before they could be used. The toys in this window were ready to be played with any time a child was ready to play with them. She gave a little sigh as she admitted that things can't stay the same forever. A thought came to her: *there is nothing as constant as change*. Where had she heard that before?

– *You need to be ready.*

'Ready?' she thought. 'Ready for what?' But the question dissolved in her head. She looked at her mother, still staring in the window, admiring its contents.

"I used to have one of those," Ros said, pointing to the little wooden telephone with the smiling face on the dial. "Do you remember, Mum?"

"You used to talk on it for hours, had some interesting conversations too," her mother smiled. "Goodness only knows who you were talking to."

Her mother gave a little shiver in the cool air.

"Shall we go inside?" Ros asked and they linked arms.

The inside of the cafe was enchanting. To the left was a long wooden counter with a glass front and a variety of ice creams behind it. To the right, facing the counter, heavy, wooden shelves held large glass jars filled with all kinds of sweets which were sold by weight. Ros noticed Chocolate Pennies and Dolly Mixtures, and made a mental note to buy some on her way out. Beyond the counter there were more sweets – large spiral lollies and sherbet dabs. There were also table displays with toys similar to those in the window and little plaques with uplifting sayings on them, ornaments and small household gadgets.

At the back was the cafe. All the waitresses wore black dresses with white frilly aprons and little white caps. Once shown to a table, Ros and her mother placed their order. Tea was served in proper tea pots with china cups and saucers, and a little strainer to catch the leaves as the tea was poured. The food was excellent and portion sizes were good. They chatted as they ate.

"Your neighbour seems very nice," Ros said.

"Oh, Gregory? Yes, he's very helpful. He helps out with the garden mainly. I make him a cup of tea when he's done."

Ros was beginning to become aware of her mother's vulnerability, and she grew concerned. She knew she couldn't just come out and ask her mother the questions she wanted to ask. She would have to be tactful. Anyway, maybe she was worrying about nothing.

"His wife doesn't mind?" she pressed.

"Oh, he's widowed, two years now. He's on his own."

"How long have you known him?

"About a year. He sold his house after his wife died. He said he couldn't stay there. Poor man. He's so lonely."

"I'm sure he's fine, Mum. He seems friendly enough. I'm sure he's fine."

Ros realised that her mother was unable to finish her meal.

"I'm not that hungry, Sweetheart," she said when Ros asked

if she was all right. “I really enjoyed what I had, and what I had was enough.”

They made their way back to the car and Ros took her mother to the supermarket for her weekly shop before going home. She stayed with her for a while, making sure she was settled and comfortable then drove home wondering just how often Mr Fielding helped with the garden.

– Chapter 7 –

"She's known this man for a year – a year! I see her every week and she's never even mentioned him."

Suzanne gave her friend a sympathetic look. "What did she say when you asked about him?"

"Oh, she said that he's 'very nice' and he's 'very helpful'. He tidies the garden and she makes him a cup of tea."

"Sounds quite sweet."

"Too sweet to be wholesome, if you ask me." Ros was in full flow. "She knows nothing about him. His wife could be in the freezer for all we know, and Mum just lets him in. You know she's not well. She's easily confused. He could be manipulating her. He could be stealing from her. I wonder if anything's gone missing."

"Ros."

Her friend's soft voice made her stop and look toward her.

"What?"

"He's not Matthew."

There was a pause while Ros processed what Suzanne was saying and suddenly realised what she had been doing. The anger and fear she was feeling for her mother was a reflection of her own life, her previous situation when a relationship had gone disastrously wrong. She had been devastated at the time. But that was almost two years ago. Ros looked at her friend and thought for a moment before speaking.

"You're right," she said at last. "I thought I'd dealt with all that."

Suzanne's voice was gentle. "Don't be upset. You trusted him. He took advantage of that."

"And now I'm angry at myself for letting that happen, for letting him treat me the way he did."

"But you didn't," Suzanne said gently. "From what you told me, as soon as you became aware of his gambling, you did something about it. It's not like you let it continue and just pretended it wasn't happening."

"That's true." Ros began to calm down. She took a deep breath. "I should have noticed it sooner though. I should have seen the signs."

"We could all say that about one situation or another. He was good at keeping it hidden. Be kind to yourself, Ros. Besides, it's your mother you're concerned about just now."

"Of course. You're right again. I just worry for her, you know?"

"I know."

"I don't know what to do."

"How was your mother when she was speaking to this man?"

"She was fine, I suppose, quite chatty actually, now I think about it."

"So she was comfortable in his company."

"Yes, she seemed to be."

"Then maybe there's nothing to worry about."

"I hope you're right. I want to believe you're right." Ros sighed. "Maybe I am making a big thing out of nothing. I'll keep an eye on Mum, though. I know there are days when she's not so good. Maybe I should go and see her a bit more often."

"That wouldn't do any harm," Suzanne smiled.

"Thanks Suzanne."

"For what?"

"For listening to me rant on for so long; for coming to meet me at such short notice. You must have thought I'd gone mad when I phoned you."

"I'm sure you'd do the same for me," Suzanne said.

"Yes, I would," she said, and she meant it, but in her mind, she didn't think she could ever be as helpful as Suzanne had been to her.

"Besides," Suzanne continued, "I had to come into town anyway. I have a birthday present to buy for my niece."

Ros wasn't sure if Suzanne was telling the truth about the birthday present but it made her feel better anyway.

"Are you okay?" Suzanne asked. There was genuine affection in her voice.

"Yes," Ros said softly. "Yes, I'm fine. Thank you."

"Good. Okay... As long as you're fine, and everything," she paused and took a deep breath, "there was something I wanted to ask you."

"Anything, you know that."

"I'm not sure how you feel about this and it's all right to say 'no' but there's an Evening of Mediumship at one of the libraries. I wouldn't mind going and I wondered if you would like to come with me."

Ros was taken aback. "Oh, I don't know, Suzanne. It's not something I've ever done before."

"Nor have I," Suzanne said. "I'm not sure what to expect but I'm curious and I would like to go just to see what it's all about. I don't want to go by myself though. If you'd rather not, that's fine. I'll just leave it."

Ros didn't want to disappoint her friend. As she considered

what Suzanne was asking and was trying to think of a polite way of declining the invitation, a thought came in to her mind:

– *Are you willing to let fear hold you back?*

The thought surprised her. Was it fear that was stopping her? She thought again about giving and receiving. She had received a lot from her friend. Suzanne had always been there for her, sometimes, like today, at very short notice. Where was the harm in giving something back?

"When is it?" Ros asked.

"Next Wednesday night," Suzanne replied. "I know I should have asked you sooner. If you can't make it, that's okay."

"No, I'll go with you. Wednesday night is fine for me. Will I just meet you there?"

Suzanne smiled. "That would probably be easiest, but I don't mind picking you up if you need a lift."

"That would mean you coming half-way across town, Suzanne. No. I know where it is. I saw the poster on the notice board at work. There's plenty of parking. I'm happy to take the car. I'll meet you inside the front door."

"Thanks, Ros. It starts at seven so maybe quarter to? That would give us time to get in and get a seat."

The two said goodbye. Suzanne headed for the High Street and Ros made her way back to work. The afternoon dragged on. The whole place seemed unusually quiet. Ros thought about her job. She had worked in the library for six years now. That was a long time for her. She didn't see that changing any time soon. She was happy there but, with Eleanor leaving, she knew things would be different, and that could be good or bad depending on who got the job. Plus, it occurred to her now that much of her work was repetitious and mundane. When she thought about it, there was nothing to stretch her imagination. She wondered why she suddenly thought that was important.

Ros started thinking of her life in general. What did she really want? Where did she want to go? She wasn't sure. She wasn't interested in the supervisor's job but it would be nice to do something a little more challenging. One thing she was sure of, however, was that she was tired of just letting things happen to her. She needed to take charge, find her own way. There were many things she was interested in. She thought of college. She could take a course of study and totally change her career. She was only forty-five. There were lots of mature students these days. But what would she study? There was nothing she urgently wanted to do. Perhaps a hobby would be a better use of her time. What could she do that would be interesting and useful? Maybe she would take a look at a prospectus and get some ideas.

She was ready for her break when the time came. She walked to the staff room, made herself a cup of tea and sat down in one of the soft, fabric armchairs still thinking about her life and where she was going. It was only as she made her way back to her desk that she happened to glance up at the notice board. One of the posters she had put up a few days ago seemed to jump out at her. She remembered having been interested at the time. She read through the information again and took a note of the contact telephone number. When she got back to her desk, she dialled the number.

"Hello? Yes, um... I believe you're running a new First Aid course in a few weeks... Do you have any places left? ... Well, yes, I am interested. Could I put my name down for that please?"

Just hearing herself say that made her smile.

– Chapter 8 –

Weekends were generally slow. Ros had little to do, now that her housework was all up to date. Although she usually only saw her mother on a Thursday, she phoned and arranged to go over to visit her. They ended up spending most of the afternoon together, talking about when Ros was little and some of the things she got up to. Her mother brought out photo albums and they remembered happy times together with family and friends. As Ros watched her mother going through the photos, naming people and recalling long forgotten events, she thought about the kind of life her mother must have had.

Ros had never known her grandparents; they had died before she was born. Her father had never spoken much about his parents, but her mother had talked often of her family. Ros knew that her grandfather had been a bricklayer and must have worked hard in all kinds of weather. Her grandmother had worked as a cleaner in one of the old government buildings probably for long hours and very little pay. They were both hardworking, honest people and her mother wouldn't have had all the nice things children take for granted nowadays. There had also been two boys in the family – her mum's brothers, her uncles – both of whom had died in early childhood. It must have been a hard life. Yet here she was, her mother, sitting in her warm, comfortable home with her china teacups and her photo albums and her memories. More than anything, Ros wanted to embrace her, to give her a warm and affectionate hug and tell her that she loved her and that she was grateful for the sacrifices she must have had to make when Ros was growing up. But her mother was pointing at someone in one of the photographs and talking about Great Aunt somebody-or-other and Ros could do nothing but look at her and smile. It occurred to her that once her mother was gone, all these memories would be gone too. Perhaps she should pay more attention, get to know some of the people in these photographs. But just now, she was content being with her mum, watching her and seeing her face light up with each recollection.

It was starting to get late but Ros didn't want to leave, not just yet. They had dinner together. Ros went out and got fish and chips, which they ate out of the paper with lots of salt and vinegar, the way Ros remembered eating them long ago and the way her mother liked them best. They talked a little while longer, then Ros tidied up and made her mother a cup of tea before leaving.

She felt tired when she got back to the flat and sat down to watch a programme on television. The book on lucid dreaming beckoned and, deciding instead to read for a while, she made her way into the bedroom, propped some pillows up against the headboard and made herself comfortable.

The bookmark fell out onto the bed but she managed to catch the page and turned back to read the last paragraph again, just to remind herself of what that chapter had been about. She was still uncertain about knowing you were dreaming while you were still in the dream but the concept had triggered her imagination. She recalled telling herself she wanted to go on the boat last time she'd had the dream and that seemed to have worked. Was that the same thing?

She read on. The next chapter talked about scientific tests that had been carried out at various clinics and universities. Science had never been a strong point. She had been interested in the early years of High school but other things had taken priority. However, she had enough of an understanding to make some general sense of what was being said. But, the explanations were long and clinical, and she got lost so decided just to skim over them. She read through the next few chapters – mainly about brain pathways and being in control of dreams – with mild enthusiasm. It was the techniques she was most interested in. To her delight, one of the first mentioned was recalling and documenting dreams. She certainly had no problem recalling this particular dream and, it occurred to her that she was beginning to remember more of other dreams too even though they were unrelated. Also, thanks to Suzanne, she now had a dedicated dream journal, so documenting them had become routine.

Ros read much more than she had intended to and it was quite late when she finally put the light out. She started to do her deep breathing, relaxation exercise before she fell asleep but she was too tired. Thoughts came uninvited and filled her head. She began to think of her mother and Mr Fielding, the helpful neighbour. She watched as, in her mind, Mr Fielding's face morphed into Matthew's face. He laughed, mocking her, before changing back to Mr Fielding. She felt unsettled. She thought about agreeing to see a medium with Suzanne. Why had she done that? This was still on her mind when sleep finally got the better of her. A vision of a witch came into her mind.

"Oh, you don't want to go there, Dearie," the witch said, her face bobbing from side to side and seeming to get closer as she spoke. "Might hear something useful. But you don't want change," she cackled. Ros felt increasingly uneasy and began to toss and turn. "Ahh. You don't really know what you want, do you? Poor little poppet."

Just as she felt the witch's face was almost close enough to touch hers, she saw an image of herself appear and stand next to the witch. This Ros looked different. Her hair was shorter, not quite reaching her shoulders, and seemed to curl naturally under at the bottom. She wore a simple dress of jade green; the colour suited her very well. She stood tall, confident, unflinching. The witch turned to look at her and took a step back.

That Ros looked at the witch and said in a calm steady voice, "I don't need you to tell me what I want, or what I don't want." Then she looked directly at Ros and said, "Tell her Ros."

Ros sat up with a jolt. She was sweating but felt cold and tingling. Her breathing was rapid. She got up and walked around her room, trying to convince herself that everything was normal, that it was just a dream. She went to the kitchen, got a drink of water and took several gulps in quick succession. She began to feel more relaxed and her breathing calmed. Refilling her glass and taking gentle sips gave her time to settle before going back to bed.

'That book!' she thought. 'That stupid book!' She swore she would take it back to the library first thing Monday morning.

After a few minutes of sitting quietly, order had been restored. Ros realised the dream probably had nothing to do with the book. She was certain, though, that something had happened, she just wasn't sure of its significance. Eventually, she put it down as nothing more than a bad dream, convincing herself that she had a lot on her mind and the last few days had been upsetting. She knew, however, that the images would stay with her for a long time. It took her a while to get to sleep when she went back to bed but she was tired and eventually, sleep overtook her.

Ros felt a bit washed out the next morning. It was Sunday and she thought she would have a lie-in. This was not something she normally did and she felt restless. Changing her mind, she decided to get up and get on with her day. Looking through her wardrobe, however, she realised that most of her clothes were basically of the same style and there was little variety in the colour. All were quite, well, boring really. She stared at the rack of clothes, all carefully laundered and neatly hung up in such a way that she could find things easily. She realised now that there wasn't that much to find. No matter what she wore, she always looked the same. She sighed. She had to wear something. Having selected a pair of navy trousers and a white blouse, she searched her sweater drawer for something interesting but could only find three cardigans, one black, one grey and the new navy one she'd bought on the shopping trip with her mum. She had pullovers but they were much the same, one colour with no pattern or decoration of any kind. She sighed again and thoughts of shopping came to mind. A change was in order. She wouldn't let the witch win.

– Chapter 9 –

Wednesday night came and Ros made her way to the library for the Evening of Mediumship. She arrived early and was surprised to see so many people. The seating area wasn't very big but a couple of men were bringing out more chairs and placing them behind and to the side of the rows of chairs already set out. She didn't see Suzanne but thought it best to get two seats while she could. She found two at the end of a row about halfway back where it was still easy to see the door. She looked around and estimated that there must be about fifty people there and more were coming in. There was a rectangular table at the front of the room with three seats at it. A lady was placing a jug of water and three glasses on the table, obviously for the speakers. Just as Ros was getting settled, she saw Suzanne arrive and waved her over. Suzanne took her coat off and draped it across the back of her chair, all the while apologising for being later than she'd expected. Ros was just pleased to see her. Within a few minutes, silence fell on the group and one of the ladies at the table at the front of the room, stood up and began to speak.

She introduced herself as Marie and gave a brief run-down of the programme for the evening. The other lady seemed to be writing something down. There was a man sitting at the far end. To Ros and Suzanne's surprise, they were to start by singing a hymn. Then there was a short prayer before Marie introduced their guest for the evening. It was all very respectful, Ros decided. At times she found it difficult to hear what was being said. Marie had a soft voice. Ros also found it hard to see what was going on and had to shift in her seat, leaning this way or that to get a better view. Suzanne was a little taller and seemed to have less trouble in that respect.

The guest was called James and, to Ros, he seemed a pleasant man. She liked him instantly. He had a gentle voice and a light humour that put everyone at ease. He was middle aged, slim and not too tall. He had a kind face and dark, wavy hair, greying slightly at the temples. Before starting, he explained that he had no control over the messages he got or who he spoke to. He could not decide to get a message for one person or another. It was up to whoever contacted him, 'spirit-wise', so to speak. Ros was quite sure she did not want a message and hunched down in her seat as James began his work.

He spent an hour identifying people for whom he had to pass on information. Some people were clearly moved by what they were being told. In fact, Ros found herself close to tears on more than one occasion. It intrigued her that she would feel this way on someone else's behalf, especially someone she knew nothing about, but some of the things being said were very moving.

There was tea and coffee afterwards and many of those attending had clambered to the front, presumably, to ask questions of James or try to get more information. Ros and Suzanne stayed at the back and talked about what they had seen. They spoke with other people who had come along, interested in their points of view. Some had clearly been to meetings such as this before and were familiar with the routine. Others, like Ros and Suzanne, were new-comers and were excited, mystified, curious or uncertain.

Ros looked to the front of the room where James seemed to

be trying to tell people that there was no more information he could give them. Then he would gently smile and shake their hands or touch their shoulder as if to wish them well.

Ros, still watching the people at the front with James, said to Suzanne, "I wonder why so many people feel the need to have information like this."

"Well," Suzanne replied, "having heard what James has said to people throughout the evening, I can see that some people would take comfort from knowing a loved one was all right, or that the person is dealing with a situation in a positive and appropriate way."

"But that's all quite general," Ros countered. "There wasn't very much in the way of distinct information like, 'The insurance policy is taped to the underside of the cutlery drawer.' That would have been helpful."

"He did tell that lady about her mother's ring."

"That's true. And he did get the name of the hamster right, the one that man had when he was twelve." Ros pondered these things. "I wonder how they do that."

"To some the gift of healing, to some the gift of prophecy," Suzanne said reaching for her bag.

"What?"

"Corinthians, I think."

Ros didn't know what she was talking about so let the matter drop. Suzanne started to put her coat on. Ros did the same. It was only then, as everyone was finishing their tea and making their way to the door that Ros happened to make eye contact with James. She hadn't meant to. They had both looked up at the exactly the same time. Ros felt a bit flustered. James was walking over to her. She didn't know what to say to him. She didn't know what he would say to her. She didn't have to wait long to find out. Suzanne saw James approaching and stopped what she was doing, interested to see what would happen. She stood just behind Ros – close enough to be with her friend but with a little distance in case the conversation was private.

"James," he said, unnecessarily, and placed his hand on his heart.

"Ros," she replied. They shook hands.

"Hello, Ros," he smiled. "Is this your first time to a meeting like this?"

Ros thought he probably already knew her answer to that but answered anyway. "Yes. Yes it is."

"It must seem a little strange to you."

"I wasn't sure what to expect, to be honest. I'm still working it through in my mind. You've certainly given me something to think about."

They both smiled.

"Yes, it can be a lot to take in."

Just then, it seemed to Ros that James' light, friendly expression began to change. It was almost as if his actual facial features changed. He took on a more serious, concerned look and began to speak.

"Sometimes things are a little difficult to understand and we often question why events happen as they do. We all have challenges in life, and they can seem overwhelming at times but we get through, especially if we have helpful friends. Challenges can shape us, change us, help us grow, progress, if you know what I mean. So we shouldn't be afraid of them."

Ros stood quietly just looking at James for a moment. She watched as his face softened and reverted to its original friendly appearance. It was hard to know what to say other than, "Yes. I'm sure you're right." All the while she struggled to understand what he was trying to tell her, and why. It was clear she would have to give this a lot more thought.

"Anyway," James was speaking again. "It was nice meeting you Ros, and I hope to see you again sometime."

He smiled at Ros and then looked at Suzanne and said, "Thank you so much for being here," before making his way to the table at the front again. He lifted his coat and prepared to leave. Most of the people had left already and the two men who were putting the chairs out a little over an hour and a half before, were now putting them away. Ros stood with her coat on and her bag over her shoulder just staring at James.

"What was that all about?" Suzanne said.

"I have absolutely no idea."

– Chapter 10 –

Ros could tell that there was something wrong when she went to see her mother the next day.

"How are you feeling today, Mum?" She was less concerned about her mother's response, paying more attention to her mannerisms and facial expressions than to what she was actually saying.

"Oh, I'm fine," her mother replied, then added an uncertain smile.

"Will we go out? We could get lunch somewhere then pick up some shopping. That's what we usually do on a Thursday, isn't it?"

"Maybe later, Sweetheart. I'm not very hungry just now."

Ros felt her concern growing. Her mum had always enjoyed going out for a nice meal, even if her appetite was smaller than it used to be. Ros put that down to the fact that she wasn't very active any more so didn't need to eat a lot. Her mother didn't smoke or drink but her one pleasure in life was going out to eat, mostly these days, with Ros and they had found a few cafes and restaurants locally that she particularly liked. On a good day, if the weather was nice, they would go for a drive and had come across one or two little hidden gems a bit further afield.

A thought occurred to Ros. "Mum, have you had breakfast?"

Her mother didn't answer straight away. She frowned a little as if considering what to say. She glanced at the clock on the wall before replying.

"Yes, of course I have," she said, a little abruptly. "It's eleven past six. Of course I've had breakfast."

Ros looked at the clock. It was half past eleven. Anxiety gripped her but she had to stay calm. She took a deep breath and got her thoughts together. She looked toward the sink. There were no dirty dishes but then, her mother always was very tidy.

"That's good then." Ros said, in an attempt to sound relaxed and ease the growing tension. "What did you have today? Was it something nice or just the usual?"

It was a bit of a trick question. Her mother often had cereal of some kind but liked variety and would sometimes add fruit or yogurt. One of her favourites was simply toast and banana.

"The usual?" Her mother looked a little confused and thought before she continued. Finally she said, "Yes. Yes, it was the usual, I suppose." She paused, still uncertain. "I don't know. It doesn't matter anyway. Why do you keep asking me things?" Her voice was getting louder.

Ros had only seen her mother angry a few times in the whole of her life. She watched as tears filled her mother's eyes and she began pacing around the kitchen. Ros rushed over to her and threw her arms around her.

"I'm sorry, Mum. It's all right."

As they hugged, Ros could feel the tightness in her mother's back beginning to ease. They stood in silence for some time just holding each other. Ros didn't want to let her go. Somewhere in the back of her mind lurked a strange feeling – a peculiar sense of loss that she couldn't quite understand.

Her mother was first to speak. "Ros," she said softly, "I'm afraid."

A pain shot through Ros' heart and she thought she was going to burst into tears. She swallowed hard and took a deep breath before releasing her embrace and looking directly into her mother's eyes.

"I'm here, Mum. I'm here for you. You don't have to be afraid. You can talk to me about anything, any time and I'll do whatever I can to help you." She took her mother's hands in hers. "Tell you what, you come and sit down. I'll make some tea and we'll talk for a while. Okay?"

Her mother nodded and complied, making her way into the sitting room and her favourite armchair.

Ros' mind raced as she prepared the tea. She knew her mother's health was deteriorating but that deterioration seemed to be accelerating and she wasn't sure what to do about it. 'Think, Ros, think,' she admonished herself. Questions filled her head and she had to work hard to separate emotion from logical thought. She took a deep breath to calm the chaos. The most obvious first step seemed to be to make an appointment with the doctor. She would have to talk her mother into letting her go in to see the doctor with her. She knew her mum. When the doctor asked her how she was feeling, she would just say she was fine, and, if the appointment was on a day when she was feeling well, she would come across as being quite coherent and plausible. No, Ros would have to go in with her.

Ros recalled what little she knew of these situations, mainly personal recollections of friends or work colleagues. She knew the doctor would most likely have to arrange for her mother to be assessed. She didn't know what that involved or how long it would take. Once her needs had been determined, he would probably look at whatever options were available, and suitable. Ros had heard of people who had carers come into the house once or twice a day to check they were all right, make sure they'd had something to eat, taken their medication, help with washing and dressing, that sort of thing. That might be something her mum would agree to, and it would let her stay in her own house. Maybe, in her present state of mind, she would be willing to talk about all of this and Ros could get a better idea of what her mother needed and, perhaps more to the point, what she was likely to accept.

Ros brought the tea through on a tray and had put a few biscuits on a plate, hoping that her mum would eat some. She sat down on a chair adjacent to her mother and took a sip of tea then leaned forward slightly and gently said, "Are you okay, Mum? We have to talk about how you're feeling. Okay? Why are you afraid? Tell me what's bothering you."

Her mum stared at her in disbelief. "Afraid? Me? What are you talking about, Ros? I'm fine, never felt better, well apart from my knees. They're a bit sore, but other than that..." She smiled at Ros but there was a questioning look in her eye.

Ros was dumbfounded. She didn't know what to say. Should she remind her mother of the conversation they'd had in the kitchen? Would that upset her, make her angry? If she didn't bring it up, she would have lost an opportunity to find out how her mother was really feeling and what she could do to help her and keep her safe.

She looked at her mother and, forcing a smile said, "Oh, maybe I misunderstood what you said in the kitchen. I thought something was upsetting you."

"Upsetting me? No, no. Don't you worry. It's sweet of you but nothing's upsetting me. I'm absolutely fine. But, Darling," her mother was almost whispering now, as if speaking in confidence or lowering her voice so as not to embarrass Ros, "we're not in the kitchen. This is the sitting room. Anyway," she said abruptly, straightening her back and placing her hands firmly on the arms of her chair, "are we going out? Could we maybe get lunch at that little pub? The one past the garden centre, just as you go out towards that big park with all the trees. Remember? We went there once before. What was it called? It had a nice feel to it."

Ros nodded. "Of course we can, Mum," she said softly, her voice tinged with exasperation. She knew only too well that the chance to talk to her mother about getting help had vanished.

– Chapter 11 –

Ros found it hard to concentrate at work the next day. Thoughts would pop unexpectedly into her mind, but as the library was busy, she would often be interrupted, and they would be pushed aside before she could make sense of them. It occurred to her to write some of them down but again, this was inconsistent and frustrating. She needed to step back, focus her attention on her tasks and try not to think too much about her mother. There was nothing she could do today in any case. It was difficult though and she promised to take time that evening to think carefully about the way forward for her mum.

– *What about the way forward for you?*

This simple question surprised her, but she accepted it as her own and gave it some thought. What was she doing for herself? What was she doing for her own future? She thought for a moment. What did she need to do? As far as she was concerned, everything was fine. She had a job she liked, a nice flat and enough money to meet her needs. She could think of nothing she needed, at least, not immediately. Then she remembered what James had said to her about challenges and change. Were things changing? She supposed they were. She had already decided to spend more time with her mother. That would be a change in her routine but once she got used to that, it would become part of her new routine, so there was no problem that she could see. And what had he meant about 'helpful friends'?

Ros was aware that she didn't have a lot of friends. That knowledge suddenly impacted on her. Was this what she had chosen for herself? She was friendly with people at work, but they weren't friends, they were colleagues. The more Ros thought about it, the more she realised that Suzanne was her only true friend. It was Suzanne she turned to when she needed help, and she needed help now. Recent events had made her uncertain. Why was there all this upheaval? She found herself thinking of James' words about challenges and how they can shape us. What was going on? She wondered if her dream had anything to do with it.

'The dream! Of course!' she almost shouted out loud. She remembered the library's book on dream interpretation was due back soon. She felt a tingle in her spine and a growing sense of excitement. She went to the computer to find that the book was due in on Monday. She would be able to take it out then. Hopefully, the person who had it on loan wouldn't want to renew it. For some reason, she knew they wouldn't. The certainty of that thought puzzled her a little, but she didn't have time to think of that now. A group of college students had just arrived. A film was being shown for a Media Studies class in the little theatre upstairs and they all had to be signed in and shown where to go.

Ros was tired when the working day finally came to an end. She was a little late leaving and got caught up in traffic on the way home. Going into her kitchen, she found that she hadn't left anything out of the freezer for dinner. Flustered, she began looking though her store cupboards and fridge, and finally put a meal together using leftover bits and pieces. That, along with some bread and butter, turned out to be a very satisfying meal. Pleased with herself, she put the kettle on and, before sitting down with her cup of tea, took some home-made bolognaise sauce out of the freezer and put it in the fridge for tomorrow night. She didn't want to be caught out again.

That evening, Ros devoted her time to thinking about her mother's situation. She decided that a good place to start would be to make a list of contact names and addresses that would be useful. She started with her mother's doctor. She stopped there. She was unable to think of anyone else to add to the list. 'It's hardly a list,' she thought, 'if there's only one thing on it.' She thought of Social Work department, but it occurred to her that the doctor would be able to give her advice about that. She had finished her tea before she added the name of her mother's bank and Citizen's Advice Bureau. She looked at the list. It was a starting point. If anything did happen to her mother and she needed more care than Ros could give her, there would be things she would need to do, legally, to manage her affairs. The thought upset her but she had to be realistic. Ros added solicitor to the list and, in brackets, wrote 'power of attorney'. How would she talk to her mother about that?

The opportunity presented itself the next day. She went over to see her mum and found her in good form.

As Ros sat in the kitchen wondering how she would broach the subject, her mother suddenly said, "Ros, there's something I need to talk to you about. I don't want you to worry, but it's quite important."

Ros immediately tensed, unsure of what to expect. Had her mother been ill through the night? Had she fallen or hurt herself in some way? All kinds of scenarios raced through her mind. Best to ask. "What is it Mum? Are you all right?"

"Yes, I'm fine, Darling. I just have some things I need to talk to you about."

"Okay," Ros said, relieved that it was none of the things she'd imagined.

"I'm thinking of getting married again."

There was a pause while Ros took in what her mother was saying. When it did sink in, she was speechless. Her mind raced. 'That Mr Fielding!' she thought. 'I knew he was up to no good!' She stared at her mother, eyes wide and mouth gaping. Her mother was staring back at her, smiling and nodding. Ros had to work hard to keep her voice steady. She wanted to hear what her mother had to say. It was some time before she spoke.

"I... I don't... I'm not sure..." she stumbled. Then, gathering her thoughts asked, "Why, Mum? Have you met someone?"

"No." Her mother spoke matter-of-factly. "But I might. There are a few fella's around here that quite fancy me, you know." She gave Ros a sly grin.

There was another long pause as Ros, although relieved to some extent, struggled to understand what was going on in her mother's mind.

"Mum."

"Yes?"

"How old are you now?"

"How old am I? thirty-seven, Dear. You know that."

This was a worrying turn of events.

"And what year is it?" Ros continued.

"Year?" She thought for a moment. "Why it's 1946."

Ros could feel the blood draining from her face. This was a new development. Her mother had never spoken like this before and Ros had to think fast.

She took her mother's hands in hers and gently said, "Mum,

even if it was 1946, you still wouldn't be thirty-seven." She watched her mother's face carefully as she spoke. It was clear that the significance of what she was saying was not registering. She would have to be more direct. "Mum, you're seventy-five years old."

"Seventy-five?"

"Yes," Ros said, almost in tears. "Mum, I'm your daughter and I'm forty-five."

"Are you really, Dear?" Her mother spoke in a voice that seemed to be almost congratulating her for reaching that age. She clearly had not made the connection between Ros' age and her own.

Ros was uncertain how to continue. She knew what she wanted to say but wasn't sure how to put the information across in a way that her mother would understand and accept. Also, she was anxious at this turn of events. It was difficult to know what to do. Clearly, being forthright was not working. Should she try to accept her mother's point of view and attempt to talk her round? It was frustrating and confusing, but it was clear that a solution had to be found and it would do no good to delay. Before she could speak, however, her mother's face took on a worried expression.

"Ros," she said, "that's not right, is it? That's not right."

Ros wanted to cry. "No," she said gently. "It's not right, but it's okay. We can work it out."

Her mother looked frightened and her eyes began to fill with tears. "Don't worry, Mum. I'm here for you. You don't have to be afraid."

Ros helped her mother into her armchair and offered to make a cup of tea. Her mother nodded her head in acceptance. As Ros made her way to the kitchen, she glanced back and saw her mother sitting forward in the chair, her hands clasped in front of her and a confused expression on her face. Her heart sank. She worked quickly in the kitchen and put all the tea things on a tray to take into the sitting room.

"I've been thinking, Ros. "Her mother straightened her back as Ros set the tray down and began pouring the tea. "I want you to take care of things for me."

"Take care of things? What kind of things?"

"Papers and things; paying bills and looking after things in the house. You know what I mean."

"Yes, I think I know what you mean, Mum. You tell me what you want me to do and I'll do it for you."

"I want it to be official. I'll have to sign something. Now don't try to talk me out of it. I've made up my mind. We'll see the solicitor and get the papers so you can be in charge. I forget what they call it."

"Do you mean Power of Attorney?"

"Yes, that's it, Power of Attorney. We'll phone now and get that Power of Attorney set up. It would put my mind at ease."

Ros' mother gave her the address book and Ros looked up the number for the solicitor. She was surprised to find it open on a Saturday. The receptionist was very helpful and Ros was pleased that one of the partners, Mr Grant, would come to the house on Thursday morning. Ros would be there; he needed to speak to both her and her mother at the same time. He would bring the necessary papers with him and, if they were all happy with the situation, her mother could sign them there and then. It was a solution that suited both Ros and her mum.

Ros considered talking to her mother about making a doctor's appointment as well but decided that perhaps that could wait till another day.

– Chapter 12 –

Pleased at how the weekend had gone with her mother, Ros sang as she sat down at her desk on Monday morning. Looking around, she saw there was a lot to catch up with. It must have been a busy Saturday. Most of it was boring administrative work but it had to be done and she liked to be thorough. She considered herself a well organised person and got agitated if things were out of place. This often happened if other people used her desk on the days she wasn't in. Just now, for example, she stood with a pile of papers in her hand and could not find her stapler. She rummaged around in the drawers and searched all the usual little hidey-holes on the desk, especially where the desk was built up higher. This was where visitors to the library could make enquiries, sign a new membership card or pay a fine for overdue books, without having to bend. Ros had to stand up at this section of the desk. There were lots of little compartments on her side and stationery items often got placed there and forgotten about, until, like now, they were needed again. Ros looked but there was no stapler. She went to the Children's section to borrow theirs.

"Sorry." Grant, the new recruit, was apologetic. "Ours ran out of staples and I borrowed yours for a bit. I didn't think you'd mind. It's only a stapler."

Ros turned the stapler upside down to reveal a label reading 'Reception' stuck to the bottom.

"I don't mind at all," she said, still slightly annoyed but at the same time relieved that her problem was now solved. "Borrow it any time you need to, but I'd be grateful if you would put it back again when you're finished."

Her point made, Ros returned to her desk and continued to sort her paperwork. It was only as lunch time approached that she remembered about the book on dream interpretation. She knew it was due in today. She checked the computer but it hadn't been returned yet. There was plenty of time. At least no one else had put in a request for it.

The afternoon was slow and Ros found herself with very little to do. Mondays could be like that sometimes. She thought about the dream book and checked the computer again. To her delight, it was in. It must have been returned while she was on her break. She went to check the trolley of returned books for General Lending and found it, waiting to be replaced on its shelf. She picked it up and read, 'Dreams: a dictionary of dream symbols and their meanings'. Perfect. She checked the book out and put it in her bag, anxious now for the day to finish so she could go home and read it.

Ros was a bit surprised to see Eleanor step up beside her as she made her way back to her desk. "I'm glad I caught you," she said.

"You look happy," Ros couldn't help but notice. "You've got a glow about you."

"I've got a date."

"A date?" Ros' eyes widened.

Eleanor tutted. "A retirement date."

"Oh."

"Sorry to disappoint you." Eleanor gave a little laugh.

Ros smiled, despite the slight gripping sensation she could

feel in her chest as Eleanor's news sunk in. "Oh," she said again, her voice tinged with sadness. "When is it?"

"The 2nd of October."

"What! That's only two weeks away?" Ros suddenly realised she was talking loudly. Lowering her voice, she said, "Sorry, I seem to remember you saying there was a lot of paperwork to do."

"All done. I only needed to give a month's notice and I have holiday entitlement still owed to me, so two weeks and I'm gone." Eleanor gave a little smile and skipped towards the Reference section.

Ros knew that the sadness she felt was for herself. Eleanor was a good boss and Ros was happy for her, perhaps even a little jealous.

"You'll miss us," she called playfully.

"I know." Without looking back Eleanor gave a wave of her left hand while pushing the heavy door open with her right. She stopped suddenly, looked at Ros and turned back towards her. "Just thought I should tell you," she said in a low voice, "Karen is applying for my job."

Ros' breath seemed to catch in her chest. She grimaced and closed her eyes for a moment before letting the breath out slowly. "Right," she said. "Thanks for letting me know."

"She might not get it, of course," Eleanor was saying. "Douglas from Reference is applying too."

Ros said nothing, just pressed her lips together and nodded. The news plagued her for the rest of the afternoon. She tried to imagine her job first with Karen, then with Douglas as her supervisor. Although he could be a bit dreary, she preferred Douglas. At least he was approachable and took problems seriously. But of course, it wasn't up to her and she would have to work with whoever got in. It occurred to her that it might be someone else entirely. Still, the whole idea left her out of sorts.

Ros bought pizza on the way home so she wouldn't have to cook. After she'd eaten, she sat down at the table with the library book, her dream journal and a pen. The book was easy to read. The front section had explanations of some of the more general dream activities like falling and flying or ascending and descending stairs. The bulk of the book, however, was a dictionary of images found in most common dreams. This would be easy. She picked up her pen, opened her journal and, taking each symbol in turn, she began to write.

Village – (country) – solid achievement
Hill – obstacle – see 'climb'
Climb – increase in status or prosperity/Success after strong opposition
Waterfall – happy rise in status and/or imminent increase in material wealth
River – (calm/gentle) – contentment and peace of mind
Boat – symbol of your life
Stairs – up is good

Ros sat back and reviewed her list. It all looked good, except for the strong opposition part. Although the hill represented an obstacle, climbing it seemed to result in overcoming that obstacle. Clearly, according to the book at least, she would be faced with some obstacle and some opposition, but she would overcome them and be successful in whatever it was she was trying to accomplish. She just didn't know yet what it was she wanted to accomplish.

She closed the book and put some washing into the machine

before sitting down to watch television but found it difficult to focus on the programme she was watching. She kept thinking of the dream meanings she had listed and was trying to piece them together. She tried to dismiss these thoughts, secure in the knowledge that things would become apparent when the time came. She thought about work too, and her mother. All the anxiety she had felt, worrying about how to speak to her mum about her health and her care had all been for nothing. She had sorted that out for herself. Ros knew, however, that things might not be the same next time she saw her. The changes at work would no doubt take place regardless of any preferences she had, but her mother's health, that was different. She suddenly felt the weight of that responsibility.

Then a thought struck her. Of course! It was so obvious she didn't know how she could have missed it. The 'obstacle' was her mother's situation. This was the hill Ros had to climb but, according to the dream at least, she would be successful. She would overcome any difficulty. She felt pleased with herself and sat back into the sofa resting her head on the ample cushion on the back.

Was this what her dream had been trying to tell her? If so, how had it known? Where had that knowledge, that information, come from? She pondered this for some time before deciding that she must have subconsciously picked up on something from her mum earlier that she hadn't realised and this was most likely on her mind, although she wasn't totally aware of it. It was a clumsy explanation, but it would have to do. It was all she had for now. It was late and she was getting tired.

That night, she had the dream again. It was exactly the same as the last time but, on this occasion, she didn't go into the shop. She continued up the hill, as before, and on to the boat.

The boat sailed toward the island and the next thing that Ros remembered was walking back down the hill. This was when she always woke up.

At least this time, she had a better understanding of events in the dream. What she was less clear about was whether she had that understanding while she was still in the dream or only when she was awake and thinking about it. Had she consciously decided not to go into the shop this time? Or perhaps there was another reason. The thought occurred to her that she hadn't needed to go into the shop because she had already understood the message from that aspect of the dream. The depth and clarity of that thought surprised her. Suzanne had spoken about the dream recurring until she 'got the message', then she wouldn't need it anymore. She thought about the different ways she was getting the same information. Not only was there the dream but she was also told essentially the same thing physically by James. It all seemed to be about changes and challenges but also about overcoming them and an increase in status or prosperity. A few more symbols came to mind to add to her list for the dream dictionary, but that could wait until morning. At least, things were starting to make sense.

– Chapter 13 –

Ros arrived at her mother's house early that Thursday morning. She wanted to be there and make sure her mum was settled before the solicitor arrived. Today was a good day. Her mum was alert and in good spirits.

Mr Grant was due at eleven o'clock. Ros hoped he would be on time. She saw her mother looking at the clock and getting anxious.

"He will come, won't he?"

"Of course he will, Mum."

Her mum began to pace the floor. "I'll be happier once it's all done and dealt with."

Just then the doorbell rang. "That's him," Ros said, glancing at the clock. "And he's early."

She went to the door and let him in. He was a young man, slim with brown eyes and unruly brown hair. He introduced himself and shook hands. Ros showed him into the sitting room where her mother sat waiting in her favourite armchair. He shook hands with her then sat down on the sofa, opened his briefcase and took out the required papers. He spent some time explaining the legalities to them. He spoke mainly to Ros' mum and explained what it would mean for her and what her appointed person could and couldn't do. Mr Grant explained everything very thoroughly and answered any questions the two women had. In the end, he said that he was satisfied as to

Ros' mother's mental state at the time of signing the documents, which he was required to be, and that Ros had her mother's best interests at heart, which was also required. So the papers were signed, and Mr Grant explained that an official letter would be sent out in a few days.

Ros' mother was clearly relieved when the solicitor left. She was much less tense knowing that Ros was there and now authorised to act on her behalf. Ros, on the other hand, felt a bit strange. This was an important role she would have to play. Although she was ready to do anything her mother needed her to do, this was different, this was a legal responsibility and she would have to make sure that everything was done properly. She would have to document all her mothers' financial transactions and record her appointments and any medication she had to take. But Ros knew she was good at administrative work so, once she got a system in place, it wouldn't be a problem. She was just thinking that it would have been a good idea to record these things in any case, when she realised her mother was talking.

"There are a few more things I would like to get organised too, Ros," her mother was saying. "Best to talk about it all now while I'm thinking about it. Do you mind?"

"No, Mum. I don't mind. What do you want to talk about?"

"I want to be cremated when I die."

Her mother spoke nonchalantly, as if she was telling Ros she'd run out of milk, or something, and she would have to go to the shop to get more. Ros was uncertain how to react.

"You're not going to die," she protested.

"Oh, not for a while, I hope. I just don't want you to have any hassle when the time comes. You do so much for me. I want you to know I'm grateful."

"I do know, Mum, but you know I would do anything I could for you."

To Ros' surprise, her mother began to cry.

"Oh, Mum. Don't get upset." She rushed over to her side and put her arm around her shoulders.

"I don't want to go into a home, Ros. Not if I can help it. I want to stay in my own house as long as I can. But I'm lonely."

"Mum, you know I can't be with you every day and I know there's a lot you have to do in the house. How do you feel about someone coming in to check you're all right and maybe make you something to eat, or help out a bit with things that need done?"

"Do you mean a stranger?"

"I mean a qualified person, someone who is trained for this type of work. Someone who is part of a specialised team with responsibility to look after people in their own homes so they don't have to go into a care home."

"I don't know, Ros. I don't like strangers coming into the house."

"I'm glad to hear that, Mum," Ros said with a little smile "I'm not sure how it all works but I assume you would meet the person before they started coming in. That way, they wouldn't really be a stranger, would they? Besides, I believe the doctor has to see you first to see what you actually need. Shall we make an appointment to see the doctor?"

Ros saw that her mother was uncertain. She didn't want to push too hard, but she wanted her mother to agree while she was still in this state of mind. She smiled at her mother and added, "I'll go with you. You don't have to be alone."

Her mother nodded her head in agreement. Ros lifted the

phone and arranged an appointment for the next Wednesday at three o'clock.

By the time all that had been done, it was already past lunch time. Ros made them both a sandwich then took her mother out to get her weekly shopping. The supermarket they went to sold clothes as well and Ros took the opportunity to have a look through their ladies' wear section. Her mother browsed contentedly but Ros was on a mission. She wanted something new, totally new, not the drab, boring clothes she wore every day. She felt the need for stronger colours and bright, cheerful patterns but was quite picky about the styles. Some were clearly designed for younger women. She managed to find a pretty blouse, cream coloured with an orange and gold floral pattern and it fitted her beautifully. She also bought a cobalt blue jumper which she thought would go with much of what she already had at home. It was a start.

Her mother looked a little bemused as Ros put her items into the shopping trolley.

"Not like you, Dear," she smiled.

"No, but I'm going for a bit of a change, Mum."

"Good for you. Have you thought of wearing a little lipstick?"

"Oh, I don't think I'm ready for that just yet. I've never been that keen on make-up. Besides, I never really go anywhere that I would wear lipstick."

"That might change, Dear."

'There was that word again,' Ros thought. 'Change.' "One step at a time, Mum" she said. "One step at a time. Did I tell you I was starting a First Aid course?"

– Chapter 14 –

It was busier than Ros had expected at the First Aid class. She had arrived early and watched as people of a wide range of ages and from different walks of life came into the training room and found a seat. She chatted with some of those next to her, while registration forms were being handed out, and found that quite a few had been sent there by their employers. It seemed they would be the designated First Aiders in the workplace once they finished the course. Others were interested in a medical career and thought this course would be a good grounding for that. Whatever their reason, they had all come to learn the same thing.

Few seemed to have prior medical experience, which gave Ros a sense of relief. On seeing the programme, however, she realised why it had to be held over the whole weekend. There was a lot to learn and she began to wonder if she would be able to cope. Then she thought of her own reasons for being there. At first, it had just been a general interest and a desire to do something practical, but now, with her mother's increasing frailty, she needed to be prepared. Although these thoughts distressed her, the knowledge that she was taking this step gave her strength. She straightened her back and got the pen and notebook out of her bag.

Ros enjoyed the first session. They were given a workbook with quizzes and assessments at different stages. They also received an official First Aid Manual which covered all the different topics in detail. It was easy to read and this helped to put any uncertainties aside. The tutor was well informed, experienced and very approachable. Ros found herself eager to get started. The morning session was quite basic. It consisted mainly of understanding what 'first aid' was, assessing a situation, and the main causes of fainting. They also learned how to get help, including what information was required to be passed on so that the response team were properly prepared to deal with that particular emergency. Although this information was in the workbook, Ros took loads of notes. She wanted to remember everything.

When Wednesday came, she told her mother all about it as they drove into town. The appointment with the doctor wasn't until the afternoon so they had plenty of time. Her mother wanted to go to the bank and asked Ros to come in with her. When they got there, to Ros' surprise, her mother asked about Ros being issued a bank card for her account. She produced the certificate of Power of Attorney, which was taken away and photocopied. Ros had to show her driving licence, which was also photocopied, and papers were signed. Then the lady at the desk explained that a debit card would be sent to Ros in a few days. It all seemed very easy and straightforward. Ros said nothing at the time but simply complied with what was expected of her. She wished her mother had talked to her about it first. As they went into the department store cafe for lunch Ros asked her why she felt the need to do this, but all her mother would say was, "just in case".

They were both quiet on their way to the health centre and Ros wondered if her mum was anxious about what the doctor might say. Hoping to ease the tension, she struck up a conversation about the First Aid course and the fact that Kath's baby was due soon. She knew her mother loved children and felt a little sad that she had never married. Her mum would have loved being a grandmother. She started talking about all the changes that were going on at work when she became aware that her mother wasn't really listening. She stopped talking and they drove in silence the rest of the way.

They didn't have to wait long when they got there. Ros went in to see the doctor with her mum. As she had suspected, as soon as the doctor asked how she was, she said she was fine. Ros gently reminded her that they were there to talk to the doctor about the things that had been concerning her, her balance and her memory, in particular. The doctor did the checks he felt were needed and said that everything looked fine but added that more in-depth tests would give them a better picture. He was also concerned about a rash on her mother's face that he thought should be checked out at the hospital. Ros' mum tensed. Until the doctor had mentioned it, Ros hadn't even noticed. But now she could see little patches of pale pink across her cheeks.

"I don't want to go to hospital," her mother was saying.

"It's just to get these things checked, Mrs Malcolm. It might be nothing and if that's the case then no treatment will be needed."

She looked at Ros, then the doctor and smiled insincerely, her lips slightly pursed and her brow furrowed. Ros was beginning to feel a little anxious as well but she didn't want her mother to see that.

The doctor explained that he would contact the hospital and a letter would be sent out offering her an appointment.

When they got back to the car, Ros asked her mum if she was all right. "This is the start, isn't it?"

"The start of what Mum?"

"Things going wrong. I've seen it with friends over the years. It starts with a little thing; they go to the hospital to get it treated and they find something else. Before you know it, they have appointments for all kinds of things, they're taking loads of tablets that they didn't have to take before and they're just not themselves anymore."

"I know you're worried about this, Mum, but I'll go with you, and, as the doctor said, it might be nothing."

"What if it's not 'nothing'?"

Ros had already considered this and she wanted to be honest. If there was a problem, they would face it together.

"If it's not 'nothing' then it's better to know now, when something can be done about it. Don't you think?" Ros looked at her mother and knew she was upset. "Let's wait and see. Let's not worry if there's nothing to worry about."

She reached over and kissed her mother on the side of the head. Her mother didn't respond.

When they got home, Ros made sure her mum was comfortable and settled in.

"I could come over a bit earlier tomorrow, if you like, Mum," Ros said. "We could go out somewhere for a walk before getting the shopping. There's that nice park, down by the beach. You remember, the one with all the lovely flowers and the little rock pool. We could sit on one of the benches for a while and look out at the water, if it isn't too cold. Would you like that?"

"It's lovely to see the leaves changing colour," her mum said, wistfully. Then walking over to look out the window added, "I think winter will be here soon. You can see the changes in the garden. I'll ask Mr Fielding to cut the grass for me next time he comes."

Ros had almost forgotten about Mr Fielding. She came to stand beside her mother at the window. "There shouldn't be much more needing done in the garden for this year," she said.

"No. I don't suppose there is. Maybe just a tidy up before winter sets in. It's getting cold."

Ros felt her mother's hands. They were freezing. She rubbed them briskly to get some heat into them but she didn't want to hurt her and softened her touch. Her mother's hands were thin and bony, the skin that covered them, like cellophane. These were the hands that cradled her when she was a baby; that held her steady as she took her first steps; that cooked and cleaned and cared for her as she grew up. She lifted them to her lips and kissed them gently. Mother and daughter stood for a moment, together, silent and loving.

Ros helped her mum to her chair then went into the hall to check the thermostat. Resetting the timer to come on a little earlier in the afternoon, she said, "Don't be cold, Mum, please. If you're feeling cold, you put the heating on. Okay?"

Her mother nodded.

Ros hugged her and kissed her cheek before leaving but when she got to the car, she couldn't stop herself from bursting into tears.

– Chapter 15 –

Ros was up early the next morning. She put the radio on while she got ready. The weather forecast was for a mild day with some sunny periods. An idea came to mind. She reached into the back of the cupboard next to her cooker to find the flask. She remembered there was a sheltered spot at the park where one of the benches sat. She thought it would be nice to have a little picnic with her mum. Boiling the kettle, she made tea, then put some biscuits and chocolate into an air-tight box and put the whole lot into a sturdy bag. Finally, she lifted a blanket to have in the car, just in case it was chilly.

She got to her mother's house about mid-morning and was immediately concerned when she saw that the curtains hadn't been opened. She rang the doorbell and waited but got no answer. Quickly, she fished in her bag for her mother's key and, finding it, fumbled to open the door. When she got inside, she called out and heard her mother's muffled response. It seemed to be coming from the kitchen. Rushing in that direction, she found her mother lying on the floor, still in her nightie and housecoat, unable to move. She was lying on her left side with her left arm out behind her. She'd hit her face on the counter as she fell, and her cheek was grazed and bruised.

"Mum! Oh, Mum. What happened?" She rushed over, afraid to move her in case she had hurt her back.

Ros looked around but there was no blood. She reached for

the telephone, dialled emergency services and asked for an ambulance.

"I came in to make a cup of tea," her mother was saying, "but I must have slipped or something." She was shaking.

"Do you have pain anywhere?"

"My left side; my hip."

Ros related all the information to the lady from the control room and answered the questions she was being asked. Yes, her mother was awake. Yes, she was responsive. Yes, she'd had a mini stroke about a year ago but was fine. Yes, she was taking an aspirin a day since the stroke. No, she wasn't on any other medication. The lady was very calm and very helpful. Ros was told that an ambulance had been dispatched and would be there shortly.

"The ambulance is on its way, Mum."

"I don't want to go to hospital."

"Mum, I can't move you. I don't want to move you in case I hurt you even more." While she spoke, she gently felt down her mother's spine, across her shoulders and down her arms, as best she could, for any evidence of broken bones. She found none, but then, she was no expert. "You need to be checked properly," she said by way of explanation. Her mother closed her eyes and sighed.

The ambulance arrived. A paramedic and a technician checked Ros' mum, feeling down her back, arms and legs, similar to the way Ros had done just moments before. Satisfied that nothing was broken and her spine wasn't damaged, they gently helped her into a more comfortable position and told her that they would take her to hospital to let doctors make sure that there was nothing else that needed attention. The kitchen was too narrow to get a trolley in, so Ros watched as her mother was wrapped in a blanket, positioned in a special chair and strapped in. She was carried to the ambulance and placed on a trolley once inside. Ros followed the ambulance to the hospital in her car and went in to be with her mum while doctors checked her. She sat in the small waiting room while her mother was x-rayed, then waited again till the results of the x-ray were available.

Ros talked to her mother but it was just idle chit-chat to pass the time. She told her that if there had been something seriously wrong, they would most likely have found it straight away and that they just had to do all these tests to be thorough. She said these things as much for her own peace of mind as her mother's. When the doctor came in, she was smiling.

"Hello, Mrs Malcolm. I'm Doctor Slater. That was quite a fall you had. How are you feeling now?"

"It's still very painful, Doctor."

"Okay, we can give you something for that." Dr Slater went to speak to one of the nurses. When she came back in to the bay, she said, "Your x-ray was all right, nothing broken but we would like to keep you in overnight, Mrs Malcolm, just to keep an eye on you. You fell quite hard on your left hip. Is it okay for you to stay here?"

"If it's just till tomorrow," she said.

"We'll see how you are overnight. Your daughter can phone the ward in the morning and they will be able to tell her how you are. Is that all right?"

Ros watched as her mother nodded and knew she must be in a lot of pain to have agreed. From the way the doctor was talking, it occurred to Ros that her mother might be kept in longer than just overnight but she said nothing. She was able to accompany her to the ward and see her settled in. She was asked to bring up toiletries and a change of clothes for her. Ros stayed with her for a little while then went back to the house to get her things. She packed a wash bag; toothbrush and toothpaste; a fresh nightgown and slippers; and some clean clothes to come home in. As an afterthought, she packed another nightgown just in case it was needed. She also put a bottle of juice in a bag and the box of biscuits and chocolate she had prepared for their picnic. She went up to see her that afternoon taking these things with her and putting them in the cabinet at the side of the bed. She had planned to go up again in the evening but her mother looked tired, possibly from the strong painkillers she had been given, so Ros thought it better to let her have a good rest. She knew she was being well looked after.

Ros didn't go straight home after the hospital. She went back to her mother's house, her own childhood home, and just sat. She cried until she didn't want to cry any more. She looked around at the furniture and the wallpaper and the ornaments. The room had been changed many times over the years. The Christmas tree had always been at the front window and the windows decorated with spray snow in the corners and coloured lights around the edges. She remembered birthday parties in the dining room and sleepovers when her friends got to stay. Her dad was alive then. She remembered family holidays with the Wiltons. They had a daughter about the same age as Ros and they had been very good friends. She hadn't seen Joanne in – she couldn't remember how many years. She thought it funny how life gets in the way of friendship sometimes. Joanne had a little brother and Ros remembered being quite envious, wishing she'd had a brother or sister too. She laughed as she remembered that there were times when she was glad she didn't. Younger brothers could be a pain.

There were a lot of happy memories here, and a few sad

ones. She didn't want to think about those just now. She got up and walked around the house, room by room. There were three bedrooms. Her mother had the big room at the front of the house. The small room across the hall, towards the back of the house, had been a playroom when Ros was little. Her mother had turned it into a sewing room years ago, although Ros didn't think she did much sewing any more. Her bedroom had been next to that. It was a good size and was now set up as a guest room. Ros was sure her mother hadn't had any guests since Aunt Irene came over from Canada ten years ago. Yet it sat, waiting for some welcomed visitor to take up residence, if only temporarily.

As she stood there, thinking these things, an idea began to form in her mind. Even if her mother got home from hospital tomorrow, she would have trouble getting around. She would need someone with her, someone to look after her and be company for her. Ros could think of no reason why she couldn't come and stay with her mother for a week or two, until she was feeling better and able to do things for herself. Although she knew she would be at work three days a week, she could be there with her mum the days she wasn't working and in the evenings. She would have to talk to her mother about it first, of course, but the more Ros thought about it, the more sense it made. She went home to pack some clothes for herself.

– Chapter 16 –

Ros woke early and was on the phone to the hospital before she had even had breakfast. When she got through to the ward, she was told that her mother had had a reasonably comfortable night and was just having a breakfast of cereal and toast. When she asked whether or not her mother would be coming home, she was told that the doctors hadn't been round yet so there was nothing the nurse could tell her. She was advised to phone back again in the afternoon. Ros got ready and went into work but found it hard to concentrate. There was plenty to keep her busy, the usual stuff, all the things she'd done day after day for the past six years. It suddenly all seemed pointless and she felt unsettled.

Today was Eleanor's last day at work and a party was organised for the afternoon. Money had been collected, a gift and flowers bought, and everyone had signed the large card wishing her a happy retirement. It would take place in the staff room at the tea break and would carry on for at least an hour so that, if the library was very busy, everyone would have a chance to see her before she left. Ros could do without it.

By late morning she'd had enough. She needed a coffee. Deciding on an early lunch, she arranged for someone to cover her desk and made her way to the staff room. As she passed the notice boards, she became aware that several of the older posters were now out of date. Why hadn't they been removed? Was she the only person responsible for them? Surely someone else could have taken on a simple job like that. Was that too much to ask?

By the time she was putting on the kettle, she had worked herself up to a state of anger and frustration. She felt taken for granted. She tried to calm down, telling herself that she was being unfair. She was just upset about her mum. Once she knew she was all right, everything would be okay. That strategy, however, did not seem to be working.

There was no one else in the staff room. Ros appreciated the solitude and ate her lunch in silence. She found herself thinking again about her life and what was important to her. She decided she didn't want to work in the library forever, but had no idea what else she could do. It occurred to her that she felt most needed when she was with her mother. Although it could be exhausting at times, it was also strangely rewarding. She felt she was doing something worthwhile, something useful.

Ros had just finished eating when people started to come in, chatting and laughing. The kettle was put on again. People opened a variety of containers and rustled packages which housed their lunches. They talked and ate and dropped things and laughed. The door opened and closed again and again until Ros could not bear to be there any longer. She still had over half an hour left of her lunch break. She decided to get some air. Putting on her coat, she went for a walk along the High Street, glancing at window displays but not really seeing what was there. Eventually, she sat down on a convenient bench in the City Square.

The town was busy. People were coming and going in all directions. She wondered about some of them. What kind of lives did they have? There were mothers with young children, students, elderly couples walking hand in hand, people sitting on the street begging. Why were they doing whatever it was they were doing? Why were their lives the way they were? She considered this for some time before deciding that it must be down to the choices they made. But people made dozens of choices every day. Why make one choice over another? Perhaps, for some, choices that should have been made were put off, delayed, and people's lives were affected by the consequences of that. Perhaps others jumped in too quickly, making rash decisions. Some, she acknowledged, had little or no choice, for whatever reason.

She became aware that all these questions were swirling around in her mind yet she found no answers. They were beginning to confuse and overwhelm her. Where had all of this come from? She had come out to try to find some clarity, some calm. Instead she was getting more anxious. A glance at her watch told her it was time to go back. She couldn't wait for the day to be over.

Ros phoned the hospital again before starting back to work but was disappointed to hear that the doctors were still doing their rounds and it would be mid-afternoon before they would be able to tell her what was happening. She was assured, however, that her mother was comfortable and had eaten a good lunch. Ros said she would phone back later but knew in her heart that her mum would not get home today. She asked the nurse to tell her mother that she had phoned and say that she would be up to visit her that evening.

Feeling a little more relaxed knowing that her mother was at least 'comfortable', she put her energy into her work and managed to finish all the tasks on her list. Then she remembered the posters. She went to the notice boards and carefully removed all the information that was out of date then rearranged those that were left to space them out a little better and fill up the gaps made by the ones she'd taken down. It was while she was doing this that one poster in particular caught her eye. "Do you look after someone who is ill?" the sign began. She thought about this. Technically, she didn't but there seemed an increasing likelihood that she would in the near future. She read on. It seemed there was a local Carers' Centre that offered support and advice to people who cared for a friend or relative on a regular basis. The information was brief but it was enough to let her know that what she was reading was relevant to her. There were details stipulating what type of support was available as well as how to contact the Centre for more information. Ros found this very interesting but decided it wasn't really for her, at least, not at the moment. She acknowledged the fact that she might be grateful for some information and support in the next few months, so she made a mental note for future reference.

By the time she had been to Eleanor's party and toasted her retirement with a glass of orange juice, it was almost time to go home. Ros phoned the hospital once more only to be told that her mother would not be getting home today. There were a few other tests the doctors wanted to do before releasing her. Although she hadn't expected her mother to get home, Ros was immediately worried. She wanted to know what these other tests were for but was told that they were just routine, to make sure there were no other issues. She was told the doctor would see her when she next came to visit her mother and she could ask any questions she had. She said she would be up that evening.

– Chapter 17 –

Ros was delighted to see her mother sitting up and looking well, although the bruise on her cheek now covered most of the left side of her face. It had turned black and she looked as if she had been in a fight.

"You should see the other guy. Right Mum?" she quipped as she approached her mother's bed.

"What?" her mother said, looking up.

"Nothing. I was just being silly." She gave her mother a hug and sat on the chair next to the bed. "How are you feeling? You look great."

"Except for this bruise. The nurse let me see it in the mirror. I must look a sight!"

"It might have been worse. Don't worry, it will heal. I'm just glad nothing's broken."

They had only begun their conversation when the nurse came over and told Ros that the doctor was available if she would like to see him.

"I'll be back in a minute, Mum," she said.

"Ros? Are you leaving? You just got here."

"I'm not leaving. I'm just going to speak with the doctor. I won't be long. I'll leave my bag and coat here."

Her mum nodded.

Ros patted her mother's hand and turned to follow the nurse. A tall, good-looking man with dark hair and rather big hands,

Ros thought, came out from behind the front desk to speak to her. He was carrying a folder.

"Hello, Miss Malcolm."

"Ros," she offered.

"Ros," he said, acknowledging her preference. "I'm Dr Thomson. I am part of the care team looking after your mother."

The word 'team' seemed to jump out at her. "Is she all right? I was led to believe she would only be kept in overnight."

"She's doing fine. Her hip is badly bruised, as I'm sure you're aware, and there's the bruise on her face, of course, but, other than that she's doing well, physically. The thing is, she's been a bit confused and we're concerned about that. How has she been at home?"

"Well I only see her once a week or so." Ros suddenly felt inadequate. "I work part time," she said, as if to justify her previous statement, then added, "I have recently started visiting her a little more often."

"You've noticed changes in her?" It was more of a statement than a question. It occurred to Ros that he must have to deal with situations like this every day. He knew the signs.

"Yes," she admitted. "At first, I thought she just had a lot on her mind and she wasn't concentrating on what was happening or what someone was saying to her."

"Do you still think that?"

Ros knew there was no point in lying or trying to cover up what was happening. It would serve no purpose and would only delay her mother getting whatever treatment she needed. Still, it felt like a betrayal. She took a breath.

"No," she said at last. "It's happening more often. She sometimes comes out with completely random ideas. I struggle to understand what's going on in her mind." Again, Ros heard herself say these things and thought she might burst into tears.

Dr Thomson's voice softened. "Don't fret," he said gently. "I know you want what's best for your mother. It's just that there are a few issues we need to take a closer look at."

"Issues? Do you mean around her behaviour?" The word 'dementia' came immediately into Ros' mind and she tensed. This was what she feared most, but Dr Thomson hadn't said that and she didn't want to jump to conclusions. It made sense to wait until the tests were done. Whatever the problem was, she would need to deal with it. She took a deep breath and straightened her back.

"Our concerns are similar to the ones we've been discussing," Dr Thomson was saying, "but there could be a number of reasons for what's happening. We would like to keep her here a little longer, to assess her and do some more tests."

"How much longer will she need to be in?"

"This kind of assessment usually takes about two weeks, maybe a bit longer, depending on what we find. From what you're saying, I take it she lives alone."

"Yes." Ros' voice seemed small.

"That's okay," Dr Thomson said, his voice calm and comforting. "We'll get Physiotherapy and Occupational Therapy involved and then we can determine what level of care she needs. It's our goal to help her stay at home, if possible."

Ros perked up at hearing this.

"However," he added, "It may be that we have to look at some alternatives."

"Are you talking about a care home," Ros was aware of the anxiety in her voice. "I know she wouldn't like that."

"Only if necessary," Dr Thomson said. He smiled as he spoke which Ros found reassuring. "It might be that we can find the right medication for her, and we can arrange for someone to come to the house on a regular basis to check on her. But we're getting ahead of ourselves here. I just wanted to let you know the situation and know that you're happy with what we're doing. Do you have any questions, Ros?"

"Have you spoken to my mother? Does she know about all this?"

"She knows some of it. She told us herself that she was getting confused. I'll speak to her after your visit and talk to her in more detail. We have you down as the contact person," he said, looking in the file and confirming her telephone number. "We will keep you informed of her progress and if you have any questions, just get in touch."

Ros smiled and nodded. Dr Thomson smiled too. Then Ros remembered something.

"Her GP, Dr Morton, was concerned about a rash on Mum's face. He thought it might need some treatment. That was only yesterday so I don't think an appointment would have been made yet."

Dr Thomson wrote in the folder. "I don't think they will do anything with all the bruising but we'll take care of that too."

– Chapter 18 –

The weekend was something of a blur for Ros. There were things she had to do in her flat, housework and laundry for a start, all the boring, everyday things that never really bothered her before but seemed now to take up so much of her time and energy. Although these things had to be done, Mum had priority. Ros took the time to go up to see her mother at afternoon and evening visiting times. In four visits she had seen her mother in four different frames of mind.

Saturday afternoon had been tricky. Ros wanted to talk to her about her stay in hospital but her mother was clearly upset and annoyed at having to be there. Ros tried to explain but her mother thought that Ros had been brainwashed by all these medical people and was starting to think the way they did. There was nothing Ros could say that would console her and both of them were getting riled. Ros had to go out of the bay for a few minutes to calm down and get her breath back.

The evening visit had been difficult. It seemed her mum was thinking more clearly and agreed that staying in hospital was the right thing for her to do. She felt that, at least they could sort out whatever was wrong and fix it. Then she would get home again. This gave Ros the chance to talk to her about what would happen when she got home. She was sure the doctor had explained everything, and perhaps her mother had understood at the time, but Ros wanted to tell her again, thinking it might be better coming from her. That's when things changed.

"You know when you get home, Mum, you might need some help around the house."

"I think you might be right, Dear, but my leg will be better. I should be all right."

"Well, it's not just your leg, is it Mum. I know Dr Thomson talked to you about why you have to stay in."

"Yes. Yes, he did."

"What did he say? Do you remember?"

"Something about building up strength in my legs."

"Anything else?"

"No, I don't think so, but my memory is not as good as it used to be."

"Well, that's the problem, Mum," Ros said, taking her mother's hand. "They think you have an illness that affects your memory; that affects the way you think about things."

Her mother looked at her but said nothing.

"The thing is, Mum, you might need a little bit of extra help when you get home. I was thinking that I could maybe come and stay with you, for a while at least, until you feel a bit better."

"That's a lovely idea, Sweetheart, but I'm sure I'll be all right. Of course, you can come and stay any time, you know that. It's your home too."

Ros was relieved. She smiled and her mother smiled back. "Oh, I'm so glad to hear you say that, Mum. You know I worry about you. It would really put my mind at ease to be with you. I'll be at work three days a week but I'll be there in the evenings and on the days I'm not working."

"Oh, have you got a job? That's wonderful. Where are you working now?"

'Oh, no, not again,' Ros thought, and her heart sank. "I work at the library, Mum. Don't you remember? I've been there for six years now."

"Six years? My, my, who would have thought? As long as you like it, Dear. But you don't need to worry about me. When I come home, your dad will be there to help me out. Of course, he'll be at work too but at least I'll be there to make dinner for him when he comes in. I don't know why he hasn't been up to see me." She frowned then looked at Ros and smiled again. "You come home any time, Sweetheart. You know you're always welcome."

Ros didn't speak for some time. She didn't know what to say. Should she let what her mother just said wash over her or should she remind her that Dad was dead? She struggled to think of what might be more helpful. She decided to stick with reality.

"Mum," she said gently.

"Yes, Dear," her mother smiled.

"Mum, you know Dad isn't here anymore, don't you?"

"Not here? Sorry Darling, I don't follow."

"Mum," she took her mother's hand. "Dad died. Don't you remember?"

"What?" Her mother was clearly shocked. "He died? What do you mean, he died? You father's dead and nobody told me? You should have told me," she yelled, turning her anger on Ros.

People turned to see what was happening. A nurse came over. She saw Ros nearly in tears and her mother pale and breathing rapidly. The nurse pulled the curtains round the bed and tried to comfort Ros' mum. Her mother started to calm down and the nurse left to get her a cup of tea, leaving the curtains drawn.

"I'm sorry. I didn't mean to shout at you. It's just such a shock, hearing news like that. What happened? When did he die?"

Ros closed her eyes for a moment and took a deep breath before speaking. "He took a heart attack at work, Mum," she said, trying desperately to draw her mother's memory back to the present. "Mum, it was a long time ago. Don't you remember?"

"A long time ago?"

"Yes, Mum. Please, try to remember."

"How long?"

Ros swallowed hard. "Twenty years, Mum."

"Twenty years?"

Tears started to form in her mother's eyes. The two women were crying by the time the nurse came back. Ros was asked if she would like a cup of tea too but she declined.

They sat without speaking for a few minutes. Ros looked at her mother, watching her eyes as she thought about what was being said. Eventually her mother's face took on an expression she recognised. She was back, and she realised that she had 'got things wrong' again. She took a deep breath and looked at Ros. Her eyes still red and swollen, she forced a smile and said, "thank you."

Ros was surprised. "What are you thanking me for?"

"Keeping me right," her mother said. "I'm so glad you're here. What would I do without you? Maybe you could come and stay with me for a while when I get out of hospital, if you don't mind."

Ros just smiled and said, "Yes, Mum. I think that would be a good idea."

Sunday had been a little better. During the afternoon visit Ros' mother had been teary. Ros talked with her and tried to settle her but she was clearly upset at having to stay in hospital for another two weeks. Her pain was being managed so she was comfortable but it was too early for her to be able to put any weight on her leg. The nurses had helped her to the bathroom in the morning so she could have a shower and put clean clothes on but that had been her exercise for the day. Ros felt she was most likely bored and feeling sorry for herself.

That afternoon she went to her mother's house and picked up, not only some fresh clothes but also some knitting and a book for her to read. She called in to the supermarket and bought some magazines and little cakes for her mum's evening cup of tea. She also bought a little wash set with lavender scented soap and hand cream, all of which she took up at the evening visit. Her mother was delighted. They talked easily for the full hour and Ros was happy to see her feeling so well. As she was leaving, she was given her mother's laundry to take home. She kissed her mum good-bye and by the time she got home and put the washing in the machine, she was feeling tired. She sat down with a cup of hot chocolate to watch television, as she usually did in the evenings, but she suddenly remembered that she hadn't put out her own clothes for work the next day. She had to rush about trying to get things dried on the radiator and ironing a blouse. She knew she wouldn't have time in the morning.

She was glad to finally fall into bed. Although a little later than usual, she still recorded the events of the day in her diary and read for a few minutes before beginning to drift into sleep. Just as she did, she heard a voice. It was a man's voice and it was coming from her left side. She believed it to be the start of a dream, the voice was so soft and gentle, but then, in her half-awake half-asleep state, she realised that it was coming from out-with her. It was as if someone was sitting next to her bed, talking to her yet she wasn't afraid.

– Ros. How are you progressing?

The question intrigued her. The voice was like that of a loving parent guiding and supporting a young child. Ros allowed the question to sink into her mind then asked herself, 'How ***am*** I progressing?'

– Chapter 19 –

Ros dreamt that she was staying in a strange house. It was an old house and quite drab. The room she was in was small and very cluttered. A narrow, rectangular window sat horizontally, high above the single bed where she slept. When she woke up, she tried to open the curtains but they were old and flimsy, and they and the rod that held them, fell to the floor. It was then that she saw the venetian blind that had been behind the curtains. She tried to open that but the mechanism jammed and she was unsuccessful. The door to the room was open and she could see other people passing by, on their way, no doubt, to whatever commitment they had to fulfil. She wondered what commitment she had to fulfil. A young woman came into her room and began bossing her about, telling her what to do. She was very abrupt and nothing Ros did satisfied her. Ros got dressed. Her clothes were dark, as if for a funeral, but the woman didn't like what she was wearing. Ros said she had nothing else to change into and the woman, exasperated, turned and walked away.

On waking, Ros immediately reached for her dream journal and recorded as much detail as she could. She reached for the dream dictionary too but realised she wouldn't have time to read it. She was already running late for work. She got ready quickly and just before leaving, grabbed the book and put it in her bag. If things were quiet at work, she might get a chance to look up aspects of the dream at her break.

The chance came sooner than expected. The library was very quiet and there was little that needed to be done. Ros took advantage of this free time to read at her desk. She could easily see any members of the public approaching, should she be needed. She got the dream dictionary out of her bag and took a sheet of paper from the printer. She folded it in half to make it smaller and easier to write on, then jotted down a list of the images she could remember from the dream and looked them up one by one.

She was a little disappointed with what she found. There was no relevant information for 'window', just a description of different types of window and the act of opening or closing one. None of these applied. Also, there was nothing for a 'bossy or controlling' woman. There was an entry for 'women', as a group but that wasn't what she was looking for. She found 'light' in the dictionary and read that it represented hope. Was she to assume, then, that a lack of light meant a lack of hope? She wasn't sure. She realised that she had been trying to find the light or to let the light in but there were barriers which she couldn't fully overcome. Also, the book said very little about 'clothes' and the entry regarding that said it was a dream of the contrary. If she'd had lots of clothes, there would be a more urgent need to prepare for difficult times ahead. It did say however that if she had few clothes or was only partly dressed, that money luck was on the way. She liked the sound of that.

She found an entry for 'room' and a bit about a 'strange room'. Certainly the room had been strange to her. This being the case, she could expect sudden success if the room was reasonably furnished. Well, it wasn't really. It only had a small bed and a load of clutter. She read on anyway to find that legal troubles awaited her if the room was empty or only partly furnished. She sighed. 'One last symbol to look up,' she thought and turned the pages till she found 'bed: strange bed'. She was pleased to see it meant an upturn in business affairs, then realised she didn't really have any business affairs, apart from her job.

She reviewed what she had written and tried to summarise. It all seemed quite negative: legal troubles, lack of hope, obstacles she couldn't overcome. Even the upturn in business affairs didn't seem relevant. The only bright spot was the suggestion of money luck. Maybe she should get a lottery ticket.

She thought of her boat dream and realised that if she combined the two translations, it looked as if she would meet up with an old friend or associate; there would be some kind of legal battle; she would find opposition where she hadn't expected to find it; and there was little hope of things working out well. If she wasn't depressed before, she was now. Yet there was talk of success and money luck. It was all so confusing.

More than anything she wanted to talk to Suzanne, but it occurred to her that she couldn't just run to someone else. She should be able to sort this out herself. She reasoned, however, that Suzanne would be able to take a fresh look at it and perhaps see it from a different perspective. Looking from the outside in, as it were, she would be able to piece it all together and perhaps come up with some insight to the meaning. If nothing else, they would have lunch together. She picked up the phone but had to leave a message on Suzanne's answering machine so she briefly asked if she was able to meet for lunch the next day. She felt better having done that. The day passed slowly and it wasn't until Ros got home that evening that she found a reply to her message to Suzanne.

'Hi Ros. Yes, lunch is a lovely idea. I'll see you in the morning when I come in but I know we're usually both free about twelve. Is that okay? How about that little coffee shop just up the street? We can get a Panini or something. Hope you're well. See you tomorrow.'

Contented, Ros began to make plans. She had things to do before going out tonight. She took her mother's washing out of the machine while her dinner was cooking. She hung the clothes on the rack to dry, then sat down to eat before going to the hospital. She didn't have much time. She liked to get there a little early. Sometimes parking was a problem and she didn't want to waste visiting time.

Her mother looked well and they talked about the events of the day. Ros' mum told her of the physiotherapy session she'd had and the exercises she was doing to try to build up her strength again. She was a bit concerned that she might have to use a stick for a while.

"I can't go out with a stick," she exclaimed. "People will think I'm an old lady."

Ros laughed and said, "Mum, sometimes young people have to use sticks as well, you know."

"Do they really?"

"Yes, I'm sure they do. In fact, I've seen them in the library sometimes."

"Why would a young person need a stick?" her mother wanted to know.

"Well, maybe they have an illness that affects their balance, for example. Or maybe they've had an accident or something. It could even be a problem with their legs, maybe something they've had from birth. There are lots of reasons."

"I suppose so," her mother said thoughtfully. "I hadn't thought of all that."

"The thing is, Mum, if you need one, you should use it. The hospital won't give out things like that to people who don't need them."

"Yes, that's probably true."

"And when you don't need it anymore, we can give it back and someone else can get to use it."

"That's quite sensible, Dear. You're right. I should use it if I need it."

Ros asked her mother if she needed anything to be brought up when she next came to visit and she got a shopping list.

"Could you bring me some of that nice juice you brought up before, please? It's very warm in here and it's nice to have a cool drink; and maybe some fruit, if you don't mind, just a mixture, not too much, though. I've taken a notion for pineapple lately, but just see what you can do. Oh, and maybe some more biscuits."

"I'll get you some pineapple, Mum. Don't worry."

"Oh, yes. There's something else, if you have time. Could you go to the house and check the fridge for me, please? There are bound to be things that are out of date now, milk and such like."

"I'm at work tomorrow but I'll do that on Wednesday for you."

Her mother smiled.

"Anyway," Ros continued, giving her mother a kiss on the forehead, "you just take it easy and get better. Okay, Mum? I'll see you tomorrow."

Ros felt more content at leaving her mother. She knew the medical staff were taking very good care of her and she seemed to be improving. Ros was finding it tiring, however being at work all day and rushing to get up to the hospital in the evening. Even on the weekend she was up at the hospital in the afternoon, then home to get something to eat then up to the hospital again at night. Although she did this willingly, she was beginning to feel a bit run down. She told herself that, as well as all the physical running about, there had also been a lot of emotional upheaval. Although that was becoming less as her mum improved, there was still all the uncertainty at work. She promised herself a lie-in on Wednesday morning and then thought, maybe Thursday as well.

– Chapter 20 –

Ros saw Suzanne as she came in to work in the Archives the next morning.

"It seems like ages since we've seen each other," Ros said.

"It's only been a couple of weeks, really," Suzanne replied. "We just seemed to miss each other coming and going."

Ros thought back. "I suppose you're right," she said, with a little frown. "It feels like longer."

"Are you all right?" Suzanne asked, beginning to get a bit anxious. "Has anything happened?"

"Yes, loads, but I'll tell you all about it at lunch." Ros saw concern on Suzanne's face. "It's okay," she said reassuringly. "It's nothing to worry about."

Suzanne gave her a questioning look. Ros nodded and smiled to let her know she was all right.

"Okay," Suzanne said. "See you in a couple of hours then."

Ros was waiting at the desk as Suzanne came out of the lift. She had her coat on and was ready to go. They made their way to the coffee shop chatting the whole time. The shop wasn't very busy and they found a table easily. They took some time to catch up with each others' news. Suzanne talked about her family and the fact that her husband would be retiring next year. They were already making plans for holidays and a new car. Ros told her about the changes at work and talked about her mother, telling Suzanne about her fall and the fact that she was in hospital.

“It was only supposed to be overnight,” Ros said, “but they were concerned about her memory loss and she seemed confused at times so they are doing more tests.”

“Oh, Ros,” Suzanne said, “I’m so sorry to hear all of this. You must be worried sick.”

“To be honest, I feel a bit better knowing she’s in hospital now. At least I know she has professional people looking after her and monitoring her twenty-four hours a day.”

“It’s a worry, just the same,” Suzanne observed, “to see someone’s health changing like that.”

“Yes,” Ros said, unable to disguise the sadness in her voice. “I can’t be with her all the time and I feel she needs someone to be there.”

“How long will they keep her in?”

“They said two weeks but it might be longer. It depends on how she gets on with the tests.”

“How does she feel about that?”

“Well, she wasn’t happy at first but I think she’s resigned to it now. I think she sees that it’s all for her benefit.”

“What about when she gets home? Will she have some support?”

“I’m not sure what’s going to happen but the doctor said he would keep me informed of her progress. Actually, I’m planning to go and stay with her for a few weeks until I know she’s okay. I can take some holidays from work.”

Suzanne seemed to think that was a good idea, as long as Ros didn’t wear herself out. Ros said she was feeling tired just now with all that was going on. They talked while they ate their lunch, stopping only to speak or to focus their attention on some important point. Ros asked about Suzanne’s son who was going to college. Suzanne asked about Ros’ First Aid course.

And then, out of the blue, Suzanne asked, "Have you had that dream again?"

"Did I tell you about the last time I had it? I went into that house that turned out to be a shop."

"No," Suzanne said. "A house that turned out to be a shop?"

"Yes, I must have told you. It was ages ago."

"Hmmm…" Suzanne spoke slowly. She was looking upward, her fingers resting against her lips as if she was trying to recall being told about that part of the dream. "I think I would have remembered that." The last time we saw each other was at that meeting with the medium, James, wasn't it? Mind you, we didn't get much of a chance to talk then. It was a busy night."

"That's true. It must have been just around that time that I had the dream," Ros said.

She related the details of the dream to Suzanne, telling her about the lady in the shop and what she had said to her. Suzanne listened intently. Ros went on to tell her about going onto the boat and all the people that were there and seeing the island."

"But you didn't go on to the island?" Suzanne asked.

"I don't remember whether I did or not. The thing is, even if I did, I don't remember anything of what happened."

"That's progress though, don't you think?"

"Yes. I suppose it is. I seem to be dreaming a lot lately."

"There's a lot going on with you just now."

"That's true." Ros hadn't thought of that.

"You've had another dream, haven't you?"

Ros looked at Suzanne and nodded. "I'm sure you're psychic."

She told Suzanne about the dream she had of being in the old house and waking up in a tiny room that was dingy and cluttered. She told her about the curtains and the window and the horrible woman who criticised her and disapproved of the clothes she was wearing.

"I looked up the meanings in the book I got from the library but the information was sketchy," Ros said, her disappointment evident. "Maybe I'm making too much of it anyway. It was only a dream and, as you said, there's a lot going on just now."

Suzanne thought for a moment then asked, "Are you happy working at the library?"

Ros was caught off guard. "You **are** psychic, aren't you?"

She looked at Suzanne who was waiting expectantly for her reply and encouraging her with a little nod.

She didn't know how to answer at first. "Well," she paused, "it's funny you should ask. I was just thinking about that a few days ago. I've been there for six years now and I've loved it. I like the work and the hours suit me."

"But?" Suzanne urged.

"But I'm getting a bit bored with it. It just seems so repetitive and I'm finding myself thinking about other things I might do instead." A thought occurred to Ros. "Why did you ask, anyway?"

"Well, a house, in a dream, often represents your life. A house has lots of rooms just as you have lots of aspects to your being. If you found the house old and drab, perhaps you feel your life is a bit old and drab, if you don't mind my saying so, and you're looking for change. You said the room was small. Maybe you feel restricted and you're looking for something 'bigger', something that will allow you to expand – not physically, of course."

They both laughed.

"The clutter in the room could be, I don't know, all the old beliefs and thought processes you're holding on to that don't really work for you anymore."

Ros was flabbergasted. She sat quietly, listening to what Suzanne was saying. It all seemed so reasonable and Ros began to wonder about the value of the book she had. Suzanne's explanations 'felt' right and, rather than a jumble of random concepts, everything seemed to fit together. This feeling intrigued Ros and she knew she would need to take the time to think about it more carefully.

"What about the curtains?" she asked. "They fell down when I tried to open them."

"Perhaps you were trying to let the light in, brighten the room, brighten your life but, didn't you say there were blinds on the window as well?"

"Yes."

"So it seems like there's something else holding you back."

Ros looked at Suzanne in amazement. In just the last few minutes, Ros had understood more than she had been able to work out in the last few days. She turned all these ideas over in her mind.

"Oh, the woman," Ros suddenly remembered. "What about the woman?"

"Well, I'm not sure about the woman. On one hand I see the woman as society, or more specifically, what you believe your role is. Are you living your life the way you want to or the way you think you 'should'? On the other hand, the woman could represent the rebel in you. She's challenging you, making you think about how you present yourself to the outside world."

Ros was speechless. Everything Suzanne said made sense. She had no idea all this drama was going on in her mind.

"Have you ever studied psychology?" Ros had to ask.

"No, I'm just a mother," Suzanne smiled.

"I don't know what to say, Suzanne. Thank you. You've given

me a lot to think about. I should have taken notes," she said with a little laugh. "I wish I could take the afternoon off and just go away somewhere and think about all of this."

"It's good to find a quiet space sometimes, where nothing else can interfere with your thoughts."

"An island," Ros said.

"Yes. Exactly. Sometimes it's good to find an island."

– Chapter 21 –

The conversation with Suzanne had left Ros thinking. The afternoon passed automatically and without much effort on her part. She was glad when five o'clock came. Her recent change in routine kept her body busy but her mind was elsewhere. She ate automatically, tidied up automatically, drove to see her mother automatically, said the same things, asked the same questions, got the same answers. She wanted to be alone, to have some space and time to herself.

When she did get home, her obligations for the day discharged, she sat with pen and paper to hand. She got her dream journal, opened it at the last entry and read it through, taking notes as she went. She considered what Suzanne had said. She also thought of the conversation she'd had with James and decided to keep it in mind in case it had any bearing on what was happening. She was now certain that the dreams she'd been having had a direct link to the events that were taking place in her life. They would be of little help, however, if she couldn't understand them.

As she read through the journal entry, she realised that her life could, indeed, be seen as the tiny, drab room she had dreamt of sleeping in. Was the fact that she was sleeping significant? Had she been asleep for the past few years? Was the dream trying tell her that it was time to wake up and be the person she was meant to be? The door was open to the wider world and she could see people getting on with their lives, but she was set apart in her little room with her outdated beliefs and old perceptions cluttering her mind. She remembered feeling as if it was someone else's house. Was Suzanne right about living her life the way she felt other people thought she should? Had she hidden herself away, become lost in her quiet, regulated lifestyle? If this was what she'd chosen for herself, then it was time to make different choices.

The narrow window that was above her bed spoke to her of her narrow view on life. Some part of her wanted to let the light in but the flimsy curtains, which were all she thought were holding her back, now seemed superficial. It could be that the curtains represented her desire to have more light in her life but they were only the first step. There was more to it than she thought. Opening the blinds would take more effort.

On reflection, she began to see the disagreeable woman as an aspect of herself. That part of her – her 'rebel' perhaps, as Suzanne had suggested – was unhappy with her life and how she was living it. In fact, it seemed her rebel-self had very strong opinions on the matter. It was true Ros was becoming discontent with her job and worried about the changes that were happening. Beyond that, she also thought about how... what was it Suzanne had said? Oh yes, how she 'presented herself to the outside world'. She thought again about the clothes she wore and sighed. To be fair, she had made some small changes lately but she couldn't shake the feeling she had when she'd looked into her wardrobe that day. It had been quite an eye-opener. She had felt drab. There was that word again. Her clothes were all functional but there was nothing..., nothing..., she wasn't sure what word she was looking for. She thought for a moment then decided. There had been nothing interesting, nothing joyful for her to wear. It occurred to her that she hadn't been out socially in nearly two years. She recalled telling her mother that she didn't need lipstick because she never went anywhere. How had it come to this?

She thought about the witch she had seen in a previous dream who had challenged her attitude to change. She thought how elegant and confident the image of her other self had been in that dream and how the other Ros had confronted the witch and controlled her power. A thought came to mind, a staggering, illuminating thought. What if that was her true nature? What if she really had been asleep all this time? What if she couldn't open the blinds because she was refusing to 'let her light shine'?

The impact of that sent her reeling. Her thoughts were beginning to merge and she felt she was going round in circles. She needed a break. She knew she wasn't finished with this. She knew something vital, something life-changing was happening.

"I need clarity!" she almost shouted.

– *Clarity? You got it.*

Ros knew that voice. It was the woman she had seen in the shop in her dream. Immediately her image came to mind and it looked to Ros as if she was ticking something off on a clipboard.

What was going on? Taking a few slow, deep breaths, she took a moment to compose herself. She was tired, that's all. It was getting late and she had to give her thoughts time to settle, become coherent. She didn't have to figure it all out tonight. Perhaps she was trying too hard. There was always tomorrow. Just now, she needed to sleep.

After breakfast the next morning, Ros went to her mother's house and cleared out the contents of her fridge. There was quite a lot that needed to be thrown away and the fridge had to be washed out. It all took longer than she had anticipated. Although the house was tidy, Ros opened the windows to let some fresh air in and took the time to dust and vacuum. When she'd finished, she made herself a cup of herbal tea, as there was no milk, and sat down in the sitting room to enjoy it. She began to feel sleepy and, setting her cup on the table in front of her, leaned back against the cushions and closed her eyes. Clouds of colour swirled in her mind, it was very pleasant. An image began to take shape and came more clearly into view. It was an image of her, nestled comfortably in the folds of the trunk of a large tree. That part of the tree's trunk, and roots that were above ground, were perfectly shaped to hold her and she felt safe.

She woke with a start. She didn't know how long she had dozed and she looked anxiously at the clock. It was all right. There was plenty of time before she had to go to the hospital. She thought of having something to eat before she left but the bread had been thrown away and there was little left in the way of groceries. She wondered about getting some shopping but thought it best to wait till she knew her mother would be getting home. She walked through the house, just thinking, remembering. She stopped at the room that had been hers. It was a good size, perhaps a bit bigger than the room she had in her flat. She stood looking at it for a few minutes, thinking of nothing in particular. She turned and looked in her mother's room. Everything was neat and in its place. It occurred to Ros that much of her mother's life was reflected in this room. She had family pictures on top of the chest of drawers, including a few with Dad in them. She had the hairbrush, perfume atomiser and hand mirror that had been her own mother's, on her dressing table, and books and knitting in a small set of drawers next to the bed. She had surrounded herself with the things that were important to her.

The phone rang, bringing Ros back to the present with a start. She ran to answer it but was disappointed when it turned out to be nothing more than a sales call. It was quickly dealt with. She remembered there were things she needed to bring to the hospital for her mother. She had promised to bring juice, biscuits and fruit – especially pineapple, she recalled with a smile. She would have to go to the supermarket after all. She would have time, though. There was a coffee shop. She could get some lunch first.

The hospital visit was largely uneventful. Ros' mum was happy and looking forward to getting home. Ros had to gently tell her that she wasn't sure when that would be but promised to try to find out. After saying good-bye to her mother, Ros was able to speak with the nurse in charge who said her mother was doing well with physio and occupational therapies. Although there was still work to do, she was making good progress, however, it would be up to the doctor when she would be discharged. Unfortunately, the doctor wasn't available to talk to Ros but the nurse agreed to see if he could be available tomorrow. Alternatively, she could ask the doctor, on Ros' behalf, about a possible discharge date. Ros said she would appreciate that.

Instead of going home for dinner, Ros stayed in the town and did some window-shopping. Much of the clothing she saw looked more suitable for younger women but she got a few ideas for herself. Looking at the time, she realised it was getting late. Her thoughts turned to dinner but as she walked away from one shop, another window display caught her attention. There, right in front of her, was the dress – the jade green dress. She couldn't believe it. This dress was almost exactly like the one the 'other

Ros' had been wearing in the dream with the witch. Ros could do nothing but stand and stare. The colour was vibrant and the design sleek and very flattering. The shop had just closed. Had it been open, she would have forsaken dinner to go in and try it on. 'Tomorrow,' she promised herself. 'Tomorrow, definitely.'

She found a restaurant she liked the look of. It was close enough to the hospital to let her relax while she ate. There was nothing she needed to take up. She had done all of that in the afternoon. She was looking forward to just sitting with her mother and chatting. When she arrived in the ward, however, she found her mother had a visitor. Mr Fielding was there, and he was sitting in her seat.

– Chapter 22 –

Ros was taken aback at seeing Mr Fielding there, and that reaction was apparent. She tried to be gracious but he had seen the expression on her face and immediately began to apologise. It was awkward for both of them. He rose, intending to leave. Ros saw her mother's confused and anxious look and she didn't want her upset. She smiled warmly at Mr Fielding.

"It's fine. Really," she reassured him. "I'll go and get a cup of tea. You chat with Mum for a while."

She patted her mum's hand and said, "I'll be back soon, Mum." Then she left and headed for the vending machines in the foyer.

As she passed the waiting area, she couldn't help but notice a youngish looking man sitting in the far corner reading. He was slim and had brown hair which held a slight curl. She guessed that he would be a little younger than she was and, she thought with a smile, was quite good looking. This feeling surprised her. Since her split with Matthew, she hadn't even considered a new relationship. The trust had been broken and she had decided it was better to live alone. That way, she wouldn't get hurt. It occurred to her now that that was a rather narrow view and she thought again of the narrow window in her dream.

She thought of all the dreams she'd been having lately and the changes that were taking place. She thought of James telling her that challenges and change can help shape our lives and that we shouldn't be afraid of them. She glanced quickly at the man again as she passed. Perhaps some of these changes might not be so bad after all. It didn't matter that he hadn't notice her. She had noticed him and had a positive reaction. That was enough. Nothing else had to happen. She smiled as she reached the lift and pushed the button to go up.

It took her about twenty minutes to finish the tea and make her way back to the ward. Mr Fielding was just leaving and almost bumped into her at the door. He was apologising again.

"I hope you don't mind me coming up to see your mother, Miss Malcolm," he said.

"Ros," she corrected him. "It's all right, Mr Fielding. I know you and my mother are friends."

"Gregory," he corrected her. "I knew she was unwell. That's why I offered to help with the garden."

"And it's much appreciated. The garden looks very nice."

"Thank you. Well," he said a little awkwardly, "I'll leave you to go and see your mum."

Ros nodded and they parted company. She found her mother in a particularly good mood.

"I wasn't expecting to see your neighbour up here," Ros said cheerily.

"Oh, he was asking me all about it," her mother chirped. "He had seen the ambulance at the house and me being carried out – quite embarrassing really. I suppose all the neighbours saw that. Anyway, he didn't know how to get in touch with you to find out how I was so he phoned the hospital but, of course, they wouldn't tell him anything. At least he knew I was all right so he just came up and asked what ward I was in at the front desk. It was thoughtful of him to go to all that trouble."

"Yes," Ros said. "He seems very resourceful."

Ros listened as her mother related her conversation with him. She also listened while her mum told her about the lovely cup of tea one of the nurses had made for her and how the lady across from her was getting home tomorrow. It was the most her mother had said in quite some time and it lifted Ros' spirits to hear her so lively and coherent. She realised that friendships were important for her mum.

– *For everyone.*

That was certainly true. She did feel a bit lonely at times. She smiled involuntarily as she thought of the man in the waiting area. She didn't know why, she would most certainly never see him again and he hadn't even acknowledged her. She was being silly. Her thoughts turned back to her mother. It suddenly occurred to Ros that her mother had very few friends near her. Some had passed away, others had become ill or frail in recent years and she had lost contact with them. It must be hard for her. She had only seen Ros once a week until recently, and even now it was only twice a week. Apart from her being in hospital and seeing Ros every day, twice when she wasn't working, her mother was alone almost all the time. That wasn't right, that just wasn't right.

Ros considered the situation while driving home. Moving in with her mum for a while seemed even more logical. When she thought about it, her mum's house was on a main route to the hospital and would be easier for visiting, as well as any future appointments. It was even a little closer to her work. With that in mind, there seemed to be no reason why she shouldn't stay there just now. The more she thought about it, the more sense it made. She could have the house warm and ready for her mum coming home, with food in the cupboards and a meal in the oven for her. By the time Ros got back to her flat, she had convinced herself that it was the perfect solution. That evening, she got some clothes and personal items together in a small suitcase, ready for the morning.

The next day, Ros woke early. She was remarkably positive about the decision she'd made. She ate breakfast quickly, tidied away her dishes and left. She stopped for some fresh milk, bread and a few other supplies on her way to her mum's house. When she got there, she went straight to the guest room, her room, and put her suitcase on the chair in the corner by the window and her laptop on the dressing table. The wardrobe was empty apart from a few of her mother's old coats. Ros hadn't brought very much with her. It was mainly clothes for work. It would be easy to go back to the flat for whatever she needed. She hung the clothes up and made her way to the kitchen. She looked around, surveying the room and deciding what to do first. She put on one of her mum's aprons and got a basin of hot water. She washed down worktops, cupboard doors and woodwork. She wanted to freshen the place up and have it clean, the way her mum liked it. She worked hard all morning only stopping at midday to have something to eat. By that time, she had done as much as she wanted to inside.

She looked out the kitchen window and decided to go outside. It was sunny but a little cool, not bad for late autumn. She walked slowly around the back garden. There were a few weeds in the borders and the pots that sat strategically placed along the back fence. She began pulling the weeds and dead-heading flowers. That done, she went round to the front of the house. She noticed that the grass could do with being cut, but there was no hurry. If she left it for a week, it might only need one more cutting before winter set in. She looked around at the houses in the street. There hadn't been very many kids her age when she was growing up and she'd only had a few friends. Her best friend, Emma, had moved away and Ros had missed her terribly. She hadn't been close to anyone else and she felt alone for a long time. She had no idea who lived in the houses now; she was so out of touch. She wondered which house was Mr Fielding's. Her mother had never said and she hadn't thought to ask.

Looking at her watch, she realised it was nearly time to go to the hospital. She sighed. She wished her mother would get home. She wished all the tests were done and the treatments and medications sorted out. She wished she could go back to a time when her mother was well and enjoying life. Ros had been living her own life too, making her own decisions, making her own mistakes. She had no responsibility for anyone but herself. That was all in the past. Being realistic, she knew her mum wouldn't get better. The best she could hope for was having her condition managed. She would need Ros' help more and more as time went on.

Meanwhile, Ros felt her life had become chaotic, hectic. Between working, visiting the hospital, shopping, laundry, plus all the upheaval at work, fatigue was setting in. She was ready for a break, a change of pace, and settling down of events, but she knew that wouldn't be happening, not for a while at least. She washed her hands then grabbed a packet of biscuits and a bottle of the juice her mum liked and went to her car.

– Chapter 23 –

The ward Ros' mother was in was divided into four bays, each bay having six beds. When Ros got to the bay where her mother had been since the beginning of her stay, she was surprised to see someone else in the bed. She looked around but couldn't find her mother so made her way to the nurses' station to ask.

"Oh, Miss Malcolm," a young nurse said, "Yes, we moved your mother into a side ward. I'll show you which one it is."

"But why was she moved?" Ros wanted to know. As she followed the nurse along the corridor, different scenarios played in her mind. Had her mother fallen, taken ill? Surely she would have been notified. Perhaps there was some logistical reason. When she thought about it, they probably did this sort of thing all the time in hospitals. She decided not to worry about it.

"I couldn't say," the young nurse was speaking as they walked, "but if you would like to speak with the Charge Nurse before you leave. I'm sure she can answer any questions you might have.

"That would be great. Thank you," Ros said, realising the young nurse would not have the authority to give her any information. In any case, it would be good to get an update of her mother's progress.

"I'll let Charge Nurse Fraser know you're here," the nurse said as she pushed the door open for Ros to enter.

Her mother smiled as she came in. Ros was reassured to see

her bright and cheerful and know that she was not in pain. They hugged then Ros sat on the chair beside the bed.

"This is lovely, Mum," she said looking around.

"It is nice, isn't it? There's even a shower, just there, as you come in." She indicated towards the door. Ros went to have a look and, sure enough, there was a small shower room which was hidden when the door to the room had been opened.

"I hadn't even noticed that."

"And there's a lovely view."

"I did notice that," Ros said, turning round and walking to the window.

Outside there was a small courtyard which held a few small trees, some flowering shrubs and a wooden bench. The trees were bare, at this time of year, although the shrubs still held some colour and there were two small evergreens in the far corner. The bench sat on paving which covered much of the area and was surrounded by lawn. No one was sitting there but Ros saw a doorway on an adjacent wall. A twist of her head revealed more paving going up to the doorway obviously providing access for patients to go outside, should the weather allow. She turned and went back to the chair saying how nice it must be to look out and see the colours.

"I was looking for you in the usual place, Mum. I didn't know you had been moved. Was there any special reason?"

"No, I don't think so, Dear. How long have I been here?"

"In hospital? About a week and a half, Mum. Why?"

"Perhaps I've been upgraded," she laughed.

Ros couldn't help laughing too. It had been a long time since her mum made a joke.

"You seem to be doing really well, Mum. I'm so pleased to see you like this."

“Oh, the nurses here are fantastic, so caring, so helpful. Everything is done on time, meals, medicines, showers, visitors, everything. It’s all so organised.”

“And that’s important.”

“Oh, yes. You have to have a routine.”

Ros thought about this for some time. Was her mother’s life lacking routine at home? Thursdays were shopping days but Ros didn’t really know what else her mother did on the days she didn’t see her. Apart from general housework, there probably wasn’t much that needed to be done. It made her wonder what her mum did to fill her time. It helped to reaffirm the decision she’d made to move in with her.

“I hope you don’t mind, Mum, but I thought it best if I stayed at your house just now. It’s more convenient for the hospital, and work, so it’s easier for me to come up and see you. Is that all right?”

Her mum was quiet for a moment, thinking. Ros held her breath, not knowing what to expect.

“I think that’s an excellent idea, Ros. I feel better knowing someone is there.”

Ros relaxed. “I’m glad to hear you say that, Mum. I’ll be there with you when you get home. I can take some time off work. You won’t have to be on your own.”

To Ros’ surprise, her mother began to cry.

“What is it, Mum? Are you all right?”

“Yes, yes, I’m fine, Darling. It’s just that, well, you’ve done so much for me, especially lately. I’m glad you’ll be with me. I don’t like being on my own. It’s a big house and I get lonely. But I know you have your own life. Some of the ladies in here are from care homes. They tell me all about them and some sound very nice. But it’s never your own home, is it? It’s not the same.”

"Mum, don't worry. I will be with you for as long as you want me to be. Who knows, you might get fed up with me and end up throwing me out."

Her mum laughed. "I don't think that will ever happen."

Just as Ros was leaving, the young nurse she had spoken to earlier came towards her and told her the Charge Nurse would like to speak with her. Ros stood, ready to go. Giving her mother a hug, she said good-bye and followed the nurse back along the corridor. But she couldn't shake a feeling of apprehension. Something was wrong.

– Chapter 24 –

A stern-looking woman stood by the front desk. She made Ros think of an angry schoolteacher ready to take an unruly child to task. As they approached, the woman turned and looked directly at Ros. The young nurse gave a nervous smile and left to get on with her duties. Ros was alert, her senses heightened. She wasn't sure why she was feeling like this but she looked at the woman, deliberately making direct eye contact. The woman stared at her and Ros straightened her back, ready for whatever she was going to say.

"I'm Nurse Fraser, Charge Nurse for this section."

She seemed pleasant enough, if a little curt. Maybe she was just having a bad day.

"I was expecting someone else," Ros began. "I spoke with a Charge Nurse a few days ago and..."

"Yes, I've been off and Staff Nurse Fairchild stands in for me." She emphasised 'Staff Nurse' to correct Ros' inaccuracy. "We had to move your mother into the side ward earlier this afternoon. You're probably wondering why."

She didn't wait for Ros to respond.

"There are three reasons," she continued. "Firstly, we've had some new admissions and we wanted to keep them near the front desk where we can monitor them; secondly, your mother has a mild rash on her face and we thought it best to isolate her while that was being treated; but thirdly, and perhaps more concerning, your mother has been quite disruptive."

"Disruptive?" Ros couldn't believe what she was hearing. "In what way?"

"Shouting at staff, refusing her medication, upsetting the other patients." Charge Nurse Fraser counted these accusations off on her fingers as she spoke.

"What! That doesn't sound like something Mum would do. You know she might have dementia."

"Even taking that into account."

"Did something happen? Did someone upset her? Perhaps her medication should be reviewed."

Charge Nurse Fraser took a sharp intake of breath and stepped to the side of the desk, indicating to Ros to step round as well so they could avoid passers-by and talk without being overheard. "She came back from her physiotherapy session this morning and seemed to be in some pain. I showed her into the side room and tried to help her into bed but she pushed me aside."

"If she was in pain, she may have twisted getting into bed. I'm sure she didn't mean to push you."

"You can't know that."

"Nor can you. Perhaps we should go and see her together, see what she has to say."

"That would be fine, if I had no other obligations at this moment. You should know, your mother's assessments are coming to an end and she will be discharged soon."

'It can't be soon enough,' Ros thought. That woman was talking again.

"I will be recommending that she is discharged to a care facility, where her needs can be met."

"I don't think so." The words came out of her mouth of their own accord. Ros was remarkably calm, but the determination in her voice was clear. "She will be coming home to her own house."

"You have to think of what's best for your mother. Who will look after her?"

"I will." Ros could feel her temper surfacing. "And I *am* thinking of what's best for my mother, and taking her own wishes into account."

"Forgive me, but I believe you are in employment, are you not? A library assistant, if I'm not mistaken."

Ros felt her hackles rise, but she wasn't going to stoop to this woman's level. "That's right," she smiled, "part-time. I can be with Mum every day I'm not working and, of course, in the evenings."

"And what if your mother needed care at a time when you weren't available?"

"I can be easily contacted."

"And are you a nurse, Miss Malcolm?"

"No, I'm not but..."

"A therapist, perhaps?"

"No..."

"Well. I think a person with medical knowledge might be better placed to make a decision such as this, don't you?" She didn't wait for an answer simply thanked Ros for her time and walked off down the corridor into one of the bays.

Ros was furious. Anger and frustration welled up inside her and threatened to burst its banks. She wouldn't let it, she needed control. Her first thought was to go back and speak to her mother but she couldn't, not like this. She paced the corridor for several minutes, trying to walk off her rage. Eventually, she began to calm down and headed for her mum's room.

"Hi Mum, just me again," she said, trying to sound cheery. "I spoke with the Charge Nurse. She said they were treating a rash on your face and that's part of the reason why you were moved."

"My cheeks have been a little itchy lately. They put some cream on this morning."

"Did they tell you that, Mum? Did they say anything about moving you?"

Her mother had to think hard. "They said I would be more comfortable."

"Nothing else?"

"I don't think so. Why? What's wrong?"

"They said you had been refusing your medication, Mum. Is that right?"

Her mother's lips tightened. "They keep giving me pills," she said, almost shouting, "pills for this and pills for that. I don't know what it's all for. Nobody tells me. And the questions; constant questions."

"What kind of questions, Mum?"

"About my house, if I live alone, do I eat regularly, who cooks for me. It's none of their business." Her mother was getting upset.

"It's okay, Mum. But you know they are trying to help and might have to know some of these things, and you have to take the medication that the doctor recommends for you. That's important. I love you and I want you to get well."

Her mother nodded.

"The nurses are only doing their job."

"I know, Darling, and you're right. It was only that one time. I got annoyed. I said I was sorry. I just want to be home."

Ros could feel a headache coming on. "I know, Mum. I'm

doing all I can to get you home soon. Okay? You just do what you need to do to get well."

Her mother nodded then, looking at Ros said, "My beautiful daughter; what would I do without you? You mean everything to me, but you look so tired. You should get a good rest when you get home."

"I will, Mum. I'll be up to see you tonight. Is there anything you need?"

"No. I have everything I need. Why don't you have an early night and I'll see you tomorrow."

Ros went to protest but her mother gave her that look that only mothers can give, so she just nodded and kissed her goodbye, fully intending to see her in the evening.

By the time she got home she was herself again. The meal in the slow cooker was ready when she got in; grateful for that, she sat down to eat. The incident at the hospital played over again in her mind and she felt her muscles tighten. She breathed in deeply, held the breath for a moment, then let the tension go as she breathed out. It seemed to help. She thought of the 'other Ros' in the dream with the witch and wished she could be more like her.

There was one good thing she had learned that afternoon. At least now she knew her mum would be getting out of hospital soon. In all the anguish of the conversation, that was the one glimmer of hope. But how soon was 'soon'? She would need to get organised. She had to have everything in place when the time came for her to be discharged. What did she need to do? The house was ready; she was ready; what else was there? Then a thought came, clear and distinct, into her mind. She would ask her mum's doctor for advice; find out what options might be available. She thought again about getting a carer to come in, on the days that she was working and wondered how to go about organising that. She would phone the doctor on Monday and make an appointment to speak to him. He would know. She wasn't giving up without a fight.

Just then, the doorbell rang. Ros opened the door to see Mr Fielding standing on the step. "Forgive the intrusion," he began. "I was just wondering if you were going up to see your mother this evening. Only, I got a little card for her, you see, and some chocolates, if you would like to take them up for me."

Ros suddenly saw how caring her mum's neighbour was. It was as if a veil was lifted from her eyes and she felt ashamed for having mistrusted him. Tired and still feeling out-of-sorts, she had almost forgotten about the evening visit and sighed inwardly at the thought. Perhaps she would take her mum's advice and have an early night. The words were out of her mouth before she could process them.

"Wouldn't you like to give them to her yourself, Mr Fielding?"

"Well, yes, that would be preferable, but I don't want to take up your visiting time."

"Well, actually, I've arranged with Mum not to go up tonight. If you would like to go in my place, I have no objection at all. I'm sure she would enjoy a visit from you."

Ros didn't know why she had said that. It was true she was tired and the headache was lingering. She needed to rest. Still, a pang of guilt ran through her, a sense of obligation, but she had to look after herself too. At least this way, her mother would still have a visitor. She would see her tomorrow when she was fresh and in a better mood.

Mr Fielding smiled and thanked her before turning to leave. Ros watched from the door as he walked up the street, trying to see which house he went into, but her attention was diverted by someone coming from the other direction. Forgetting about Mr Fielding, she turned to look. A man, youngish-looking, slim with brown hair walked past on the far side. He didn't look over at her but, for one moment, he made her think of the man she had seen in the hospital waiting room.

– Chapter 25 –

Ros went to the hospital early the next day. Being a Sunday, she knew her chances of seeing a doctor were slim but she might be able to speak with someone in authority, someone who could give her some insights about the procedures that had to be followed for her mum's release. She found no one. She sat in the cafe while she drank coffee and ate a pastry with strawberries and whipped cream. It was an indulgent treat and she enjoyed it.

"Oh Ros. I'm so glad to see you," her mother called as she walked in the door. Her mum was dressed and sitting up in a large chair next to her bed.

Ros misunderstood the urgency in her voice and was concerned. "Are you all right, Mum?" she asked, rushing over to her side.

"Yes, I'm fine," she beamed. "You'll never guess."

"What is it, Mum?"

"I'm getting home! Isn't that wonderful? I'm finally getting home."

Ros was immediately concerned. What had her mother been told? Who had told her and why? Had a definite decision been made? Why had she not been informed? She didn't want to say the wrong thing and upset her mum, or jump to any conclusions, but she really needed to know what was going on.

"That's wonderful," she said, forcing a smile. "When did you find out?"

"Just this morning."

"Did the doctor tell you?"

"No. It was someone else."

"Was it a nurse, Mum?"

"I'm not sure. It might have been."

"Do you remember which one? I'd like to speak to her."

"Oh dear, I don't know. It was an older woman. She said that since I was doing so well with all my treatments and such, it was likely I would be discharged soon."

"Well, we talked about that yesterday, Mum. Remember we said the doctor has to say it's okay first."

"Can't you take me home now?"

"Mum, I would love to but we have to wait till the doctor tells you, and the doctor has to know you're well enough to leave the hospital."

Her mother's expression darkened.

"Tell you what. I'll see if I can find someone to ask before I leave, see if I can get more information."

Although disappointed, this satisfied her mother and she seemed content to wait. Ros asked no more questions. She was confused, however, why anyone would even mention getting home to her mother if nothing had been decided about where she would be going. And why say 'getting home', if there was a chance that she might not be going to her own house? Ros had initially been angry at the Charge Nurse for this, but had to accept that it may not have been her. Perhaps it had been mentioned to another nurse who had, in turn, mentioned it to her mum, thinking it would cheer her up. Regardless of the circumstances, this news should have come from the doctor, surely. She was happy to see her mum so excited and positive, but she needed to be sure that her mother had not simply misunderstood what had been said. She decided not to get upset about it. For all she knew, it could have simply been a conversation with another patient.

On her way out, Ros looked around for someone to talk to at the nurses' station. It was a busy place and all the staff seemed occupied. She spied a young woman wearing a white coat and an ID badge on a lanyard round her neck whom she thought might be able to help. Ros rushed up to her.

"Excuse me, Dr..."

"Dr Simpson," the woman smiled and moved her glasses to the top of her head. "I just popped in to see a patient, actually, but, yes, how can I help you?"

"I'm sorry to bother you. I just wondered if you could answer a question for me. My mother has just told me she is due to be discharged. I know nothing about it and I just wondered if she is, in fact, being discharged and if a date had been set. Sorry, I don't know what the procedures are."

"Oh, I see. Well, I could try to find out for you."

Ros gave her mother's name and followed Dr Simpson to the desk. Ros watched as she looked through folders and checked the calendar.

"Her case is being reviewed and she is being considered for discharge but no date has been set as yet, Miss Malcolm. There has to be a meeting first anyway to decide when a patient is ready to be discharged and where they are discharged to. If it's not to a care facility, then a care package has to be put in place. They are not just let out the door and left to get on with it, if you know what I mean."

She gave a little laugh and Ros laughed too.

"And who decides what happens?"

"It's a multi-disciplinary meeting, so there will be medical and nursing staff, social work, and an Occupational Therapist. As a relative, you can be there too."

Ros could feel excitement growing. "Do I have a say? Can I put ideas forward?"

"Oh, yes. You obviously want what's best for your mother, and so do we, of course, but it's good to have a well-informed discussion."

This was exactly what Ros needed to know. "Thank you so much," she said. "I really appreciate your help. Oh, just one more thing. Is there a date for the meeting?"

"Yes, I thought you'd ask." She handed Ros a slip of paper. "It's not this Friday but next, the 23rd at 10:00, in the small meeting room at the end of the ward."

Ros thanked her again and went back to her mother to let her know.

Plans formulated in her head as she made her way home. She had things to do and less than two weeks to do it. She had to be ready.

Ros had stayed with the same medical practice as her mother. She phoned the surgery the next day and was told there was a cancellation on Wednesday morning, if that wasn't too short notice. Ros said it was perfect and thanked the receptionist. She felt good and breezed through the morning with barely a thought of work, her focus was getting her mother home. Things seemed to be falling into place quite nicely.

Although it had only been a few days, Ros was feeling settled in her old bedroom. She loved being back home again and realised how much she had missed the house and the street and the memories.

Although much of Ros' time was spent either at work or at the hospital, there was little for her to do when she was in the house. She didn't have a lot of books but now missed them and decided to call into her flat tomorrow to pick some up. More clothes might be an idea too. Thinking again about her clothes, she remembered the green dress and mentally put that on her list for tomorrow as well.

– Chapter 26 –

Work was quiet during the morning, until the memo came. The interviews for Eleanor's job had taken place and, Karen, her new supervisor would start work on the second of November. Ros closed her eyes and sighed heavily. She had hoped someone else would be chosen. She dreaded the thought of having Karen hovering over her, double-checking everything she did and picking her up on the tiniest detail. She sighed again. She had a couple of weeks to get used to the idea. Maybe it wouldn't be that bad. In any case, she had no choice; she would just have to cope. Then she remembered something that would cheer her up.

At her lunch break Ros walked down the High Street to the shop where she had seen the green dress. It was still on display in the window and she hadn't changed her mind about it. She went inside and glanced around but couldn't see it. Her time was limited so she asked an assistant for help. The young woman, more a girl really, took her further along to a row against the back wall where the dress could be found, asked her size, selected one from the rail and led her to the changing rooms.

Ros put the dress on and stood transfixed in front of the full-length mirror. No words came to mind; she stared at the image and let its effects seep in before she could even try to think of words. When conscious thought returned, she tried to analyse what she felt. She found this difficult but realised something fundamental – the colour of the dress seemed to brighten her face, changing her appearance totally. It was as if another person was staring back at her. Never had a dress fitted her so perfectly. It could almost have been made just for her. She stood looking for some time, feeling stronger and more confident; a curious feeling but she liked it. She looked and felt amazing but something wasn't right.

After a moment's consideration, she decided that it was her hair. This was odd. She had liked her hair that morning. What was different? She had always worn it up, or sometimes tied back, more to have it out of the way than for any other reason. But now, it just didn't suit. If she was to be taken seriously, she had to get this right. She suddenly realised that if she was always trying to get it out of the way, maybe it should be shorter. Reaching up she pulled at the clasps and bobbles that held it in place. They came away easily and her long auburn hair flowed over her shoulders and down her back to just below the shoulder blades. That was better, but still not right. She gathered it up again, loosely in her hand, ponytail style, and holding it close to the back of her head to start with, slowly softened her grasp allowing the hair to fall through. She drew her hand down until the hair sat just above her shoulders. She stopped there, holding it in place, taking in its effect. She liked it. She liked it a lot.

Ros couldn't remember the last time she had been to a hairdresser, for anything more than a trim, and she was uncertain about new styles and what to ask for. The girls at work would know. She would ask one or two of them, discreetly, when she got back. She changed back into her work clothes, paid for the dress and made her way along the High Street.

Ros looked around as she walked to her desk, taking note of people milling about. Although mainly interested in the different hair styles women had, she also picked up on fashion ideas, clothing and accessories. As she sat down, Jacquie approached her.

"Hi, Ros. Got some paperwork for you. As if you don't have enough, right?"

"No problem, Jacquie, thanks."

Ros noticed that Jacquie had a simple hairstyle that looked easy to manage. "Can I ask you a question? Do you mind?"

"Sure. Go for it."

"I'm thinking of doing something different with my hair and, well, yours always looks so nice. Can I ask where you go to get it cut?"

"Ahh, thanks Ros, that's really nice. I go to a salon close to where I live. I could give you their number if you like. What kind of style are you looking for?"

"Well, that's the problem. I'm not really sure."

It was exactly at that point that Sue, from the video library came by and picked up on the conversation. Soon others turned to see what was going on.

Ros tried to be nonchalant, saying she was just toying with the idea of getting a new style, but the fact that she was asking at all caused a buzz amongst her co-workers. They flocked to her, offering advice on the type of cut she should have, which salon to go to, which stylist to ask for and even suggesting she change the colour. Ros wasn't ready for that, not yet anyway. She took on board all that they said and deciding on something simple and easy to look after, phoned a local salon and made an appointment. It was the only way she could stop the flood of suggestions coming her way.

On her way to her mother's house, Ros called into her flat for the things she needed. When she got in, she found a lot of mail lying in the hall. Picking it up and flicking through it, she decided it was mostly junk mail and set it on the hall table. When she looked, there, sitting on the top of the pile, was a leaflet for the local Carers' Centre. She stood looking at it for several seconds. That was odd. This was the second time the name had caught her attention. Trusting her instincts, she picked it up and put it in her bag. She would read it later.

Her bookcase didn't have a very big selection of books but she chose a few to take with her, making a mental note to expand her reading horizons. Having picked up some fresh clothes, she was soon ready to leave. She was beginning to think of her mother's house as 'home'.

Wednesday came and her visit to the doctor went very well. He was able to give her advice on the different types of help that were available and discussed those which might best meet her mother's needs. He also gave her some ideas of what questions to ask when she went to the meeting, and what points to put across. Armed with this information, Ros felt ready. There was just one more thing she had to do. She went shopping again and found a blouse with a subtle, sage-coloured, leaf pattern and a sweater that matched the colour of the leaves exactly. She decided she liked green.

– Chapter 27 –

That night Ros had the dream again. Everything was familiar, up to a point. The boat set sail, as before; she went outside on the upper deck, as before; and she saw the island, as before. This time there was more. This time she watched, mesmerised as the island grew larger in front of her. Her excitement grew with it.

As it started to come into focus, Ros tried to determine shapes, considering what she might find when she finally stepped on shore. At that moment, an unusual and unexpected sensation enveloped her. Perhaps it was her imagination, but it was too strong to ignore. She had the distinct impression that the island was welcoming her and she felt exhilarated.

It didn't look very big, perhaps only three or four miles long. As they approached, she strained to make out specific structures but the sun was behind the island and much of detail was lost. The only discernible feature was the small, ragged mountain that sat in the centre and dominated the skyline. As they approached, more of the island's mysteries revealed themselves and Ros could see a stony beach where a long, concrete jetty stretched out to meet them. It looked the perfect height to reach the lower deck of the boat and the metal barrier that allowed people to embark and disembark. She also noticed a wooded area off to the right. As the boat drew nearer, her anticipation grew and the more excited she became.

They pulled alongside the jetty and the engines stopped. Ros found she missed the sound they made. She was uncertain of what to do next. Did they just get off the boat? Did they have to wait for an announcement to be made? When she thought about it, there had been no instructions for any aspect of this journey. She looked around at the other passengers, intent on following their lead. Most were still standing, looking out, pointing and talking. Had they been here before, or was it a first time for everyone? Others started moving, making their way downstairs. Ros followed them inside. She reached the lower deck and, walking past the little table where she had first sat with her coffee, continued out the door with the crowd, down the gangplank and on to the jetty.

It was only a short walk to where the jetty became the road and when Ros got to that point she stopped and took in her surroundings. The water was the most beautiful shade of turquoise she had ever seen. It was crystal clear, with a white, lacy, foam edge where it met the shore. The beach was mostly sand littered with driftwood and seaweed. A ribbon of small stones and shells divided it, almost exactly in half, between the water and the dunes.

She stood, watching, waiting to see what would happen. Everyone seemed to be off the boat and, to her amazement, they kept walking as if they knew where they wanted to go. Ros didn't know where she wanted to go. She looked around, not knowing which direction to take. 'I need guidance', she thought.

– *'Guidance' – check.*

It was the woman's voice again, the one from the shop, and although Ros didn't have an image of her as before, she imagined her ticking something off on her clipboard, and smiled at the thought.

As the crowd thinned, her attention was drawn to a path that led off to the right and towards the trees. Ros felt a strong urge to follow it and, although uncertain at first, decided that she should trust whatever feelings she had while she was here. She walked, alone, into the grove.

The early morning sun shone through the leaves making a dappled pattern on the ground. There were trees of almost every size and shape. They were all clothed in brilliant green, and a million buds. Some were already beginning to open and all held the promise of colourful and abundant blossom. A gentle breeze flexed their boughs, the lower ones almost brushing against her as she walked by, as if trying to touch her. Birds darted here and there looking for food or materials to build their nests.

There were flowers too, bushes, climbing things and a myriad of other plant life. Small, green shoots were gently making their way above ground. Looking down, Ros noticed a little shoot growing out from under a heavy stone. Instinctively she lifted the stone to see the small stem misshapen and growing at an angle. Ros realised that the stone had been blocking the plant's growth but it had worked its way around the stone and found another route in order to flourish. This thought captured her attention and she wondered what motivated something to grow despite the odds. The next question that came to mind was more difficult. What was blocking her growth? She didn't know. She carried the question with her as she placed the stone back on the ground, away from the little plant, and continued walking.

The air was fresh and clean, and everything felt new. Ros closed her eyes and let the feeling refresh her. As she followed the path she came to a large oak tree, set alone in a clearing. It was bigger than the others and had a heavy trunk. Ros guessed that it was as tall as the block of flats she lived in, maybe even taller. She had to bend her head right back to see where it reached. She stretched out her arms but her span did not reach half the trunk's circumference. Intrigued, she walked around its base and stopped suddenly when she got to the other side. There in the configuration of the roots that were above ground, and the shape of the folds in its trunk at that particular point, was the tree she had seen in one of her dreams. It had cradled her and she had felt safe, protected and loved. Perhaps more to the point, she now felt worthy of that love. Without thinking, she curled into the space the tree provided, positioning herself in its curves as those feelings returned. She wept soft tears as she realised the love she felt was for herself, and she was suddenly aware that she, as an individual, mattered.

She rested there for a time, feeling like a child again being held in the arms of a loving parent, perhaps even in the womb. When she opened her eyes she knew that something significant had happened, the feeling was so intense. She felt strength, in all its manifestations, rising in her. She could see her way forward. It was as if her body, mind and spirit had been reinforced, realigned. She felt different and yet completely natural, as if this power had always been part of her but she had been unaware of it. A new chapter was opening in her life and there was purpose in it. Challenges were coming but somehow, she knew she could adapt and could trust her inner guidance to make the right decisions. This was new territory for her but she was ready to take on whatever came her way. She saw the branches bend and sway in a gentle breeze and admired their resilience. She rose and, gently placing her hand on the trunk of the tree, silently thanked it for the healing message of renewal, growth and flexibility it had given her.

As she walked, the trees gently gave way to a wildflower meadow. The heady scent of wild garlic mixed with the sweetness of the flowers and she breathed deeply. She saw a few fruit trees as she passed. The fruit seemed almost ripe enough to eat. Strange that she hadn't even thought of food since this journey began. Reaching up, she plucked a cherry and put it in her mouth. It was bitter and hard, and she spat it out. Clearly it needed more time to mature. It occurred to her that this orchard was not like others she had seen before, with neat rows and clear divisions. These trees had the look of having grown wherever the seed had fallen, as if scattered by some unseen hand.

There were bushes and vines of every description. The garden was bursting with life, vibrant with colour, fragrance, heat and light, everything to stir the senses. It was a beautiful day, a perfect day. It made her think of a time long ago when she was young and life was an adventure. Somehow that vibrancy, that zest for life had been set aside. She walked further noticing everything; colours, shapes, smells and sounds. Multi-coloured butterflies filled the air, insects buzzed, birds sang and every growing thing was in full bloom. She drank it all in, allowing it to become part of her.

The bright sun warmed her skin and she closed her eyes. Feeling light and carefree, and taking off her shoes, she walked on the grass in her bare feet, something she hadn't done since childhood. The grass was cool despite the sun's heat. She ran through the tall grass sending clouds of dandelion flying in her wake. Her heart quickened and she felt her spirit soar. Exuberant, she opened her arms and spun around in a circle. When she began to feel giddy, she stopped and looked around. A slight sadness caught her unawares. This place contained an abundance of life yet there were no other people, no one to share this amazing experience with. She thought of all the people she had seen on the boat. Everyone had been with someone else, some even in family groups, everyone except her. That was going to change. A lot was going to change.

She walked on, the heat and the light distracting her and softening her mood. The scent of sweet roses, lavender and honeysuckle filled her head and she lay down on the grass to let her mind wander. It felt strange, daydreaming while she was in a dream. Was that music she could hear somewhere in the distance? Its steady rhythm roused her and she sat up, listening carefully, but it was gone. Had it just been birdsong; just the hum of insects or the wind rustling through the flowers? Surely not. Yet there was nothing else. She lay down again and closed her eyes. The music was back but it was subtle, just out of reach. She let it play in her head then laughed at the thought that it was her own heartbeat; the song of her soul.

– Chapter 28 –

Ros didn't know how long she had been lying there but the sun had moved from its zenith. She stood up and stretched her arms and back. The path appeared to open again in front of her and she made her way towards it. As she followed its twists and turns, the wildflowers of the meadow faded away and were replaced by rows of neat houses with well-kept lawns. Beyond the houses was an open green. There were people everywhere, gathered in small groups, some sitting on the grass with their picnics, while children ran and played. Others sat at tables, or walked along the grass talking and playing games with the children. She caught a gentle scent of freshly baked bread, reminding her of home long ago when she and her mother would spend the day baking. Were these people all part of the same family, the same community? She wasn't sure. Clearly, they knew each other. Someone turned as she approached.

"Ah, Ros. We've been waiting for you. Come on over and sit with us."

Ros was aghast. Who was this woman and how did she know her name? Still, it was a warm welcome and she was happy to have company. The woman sat up on the blanket making room for Ros to sit beside her. There were three other adults with her, one woman and two men. Ros guessed they were all about the same age. The woman held out a shallow basket with, not only freshly-baked bread but also an inviting mixture of fruits and vegetables. There was nothing in packages. They all looked fresh and ripe, as if they had just been picked off the vine, or a nearby tree, only moments before. Reaching out, Ros took a large, red berry and placed it in her mouth. The taste was exceptional. She ate it slowly and as she swallowed, she felt as if the flavour filled her whole body.

The people she sat with were pleasant company and, as they chatted, others turned to see what was happening. There were shouts of 'Hi Ros' and 'Haven't seen you for a while'. Although Ros didn't recognise anyone, she had an overwhelming sense of belonging and waved back. It warmed her heart to have such a friendly welcome.

"This is wonderful," Ros said. "Everyone seems to know me."

"And that surprises you?"

"Well, yes," she said, a little embarrassed. "I don't remember being here before."

"That's perfectly understandable," one man said.

"It doesn't change anything," the other woman said. "We still love you."

Ros was caught off guard and could feel her eyes begin to sting. Why should being loved make her want to cry? The fact that these people knew her and loved her was a lot to take in. She managed to set the urge aside, but she wasn't sure what her feelings were; acceptance certainly, but there was more, a deep, sincere friendship and a regard for the people and, what seemed like a very gentle way of life. She struggled to find the right word. 'Connection', that's what it was. She felt connected to this place and to the people around her. A slight sadness washed over her as she wondered how she had become disconnected.

"What have you seen so far," the first woman wanted to know.

Ros conveyed all that she had seen, heard and even smelt. The next question was different.

"And how did it make you feel?" the other woman asked.

A small group had gathered and sat with them. Ros was happy to have them join in.

"I love this place," she said. "I feel so relaxed and at-home. I need to keep this sense of being part of everything that's happening around me. I know I contribute to that, in lots of different ways, but others do too. I think I'd forgotten that."

She wasn't sure where all the words had come from but they sounded right and were sincere.

"And you take what you need from it as well," someone added. "It's a two-way process."

"Sounds like you're lacking vitamin R," said an older man.

"Vitamin R?" she'd never heard of that one.

"R for Ros." His voice was gentle and full of concern. It also sounded familiar but she couldn't think where she would have heard it before.

When she thought about it, she realised that she hadn't been very conscious of her own needs. She had shut herself away and denied the love and care offered by those around her. She hadn't 'honoured' herself. Just acknowledging that seemed to shift something deep inside her. How had she become so numb? She had built a wall to protect herself, to keep others out but it had also locked her in. Ros dropped her gaze.

The man came to her rescue. "There will always be choices to make. There will always be jobs to do and commitments to be fulfilled, and sometimes it doesn't seem like you have a lot of choice. But your approach, your attitude, will make all the difference."

Ros considered his words and found truth in them.

"Is this your first time to the island?" he asked.

That was tricky. Although Ros had had the dream several times, this was the first time she remembered actually being on the island. Surely, a place such as this she would have remembered. Then a thought occurred to her. Were the others dreaming too? Was this nothing more than her imagination? She didn't think she was that creative.

She turned to the man. "Yes, it is, as far as I can remember," she said. It was the most honest answer she could give. "And you?" she asked.

"This is my home."

Something resonated with Ros as he spoke and she wasn't sure how to respond.

"It's okay," he said. "We knew you would be coming and we've been waiting for you. On your first visit you'll go through all the areas in a particular order. After that, you can come back any time you want and go to the place that is most relevant for whatever you need at the time."

"I'm not sure I understand." Ros was aware that the others had begun different conversations with each other. Groups had changed as individuals turned to talk to someone else, or walk to a different part of the park. The man stood and began walking, his pace casual. Ros walked alongside.

"How did you feel when you were in the wooded area?"

"I felt that I had purpose in my life," she blushed a little at hearing herself say that. "But it's more than that," she continued. "Now that I think about it, it's like I have the courage to move forward, to make decisions and 'go with the flow.'" Ros spread her hands out in front of her as she spoke.

The man smiled. "Good," he said, "That's the nature of trees, bending with the winds. Anything else?"

Ros tried to recall. She had relaxed so much and accepted so much of what was happening that now she was being asked to identify her feelings and analyse them, she was struggling. She closed her eyes and let the words come naturally.

"I suppose, if I'm honest, I had a sense of..." She paused. "Don't laugh," she said, pointing a finger playfully at him, "I suppose I had a sense of renewal; almost like someone had pushed my reset button. I know that sounds daft."

"It's not daft at all. I knew you were astute. You thanked the tree for its message. That shows gratitude. That's very powerful, and it shows that you are aware of your connection with other living things."

'How had he known that?' she wondered.

"We're all connected," he said, answering her silent question.

Ros gave an embarrassed smile. He gave her a warm and understanding smile in return.

"What about the next area you visited?"

Ros had to think to remember. "Oh, yes, the garden. It was so warm and vibrant with colour, fragrance, birdsong. I loved that. I got strength from that, self-confidence too.

The man smiled.

"You're going to ask me about this last experience, aren't you?"

Ros answered before the man had time to reply, even though he made no effort to do so.

"I feel very mellow – no, 'balanced' would be a better word. I loved having people round me and the people here accepted me and welcomed me in. I've locked myself away for so long I've forgotten what it's like to be part of anything. I guess I really was 'out of balance'".

"You weren't 'accepted', you are already part of the company, part of this community. You always have been."

Ros was confused but the man carried on. “These people are part of your family. You may not know them in waking life but they know you and, on another level, you know them as well. You are welcome here, Ros. You will always be welcome. Open yourself up to the possibility of new communities, new friendships. You love interacting with people, allow yourself to do that, not just for your sake but for theirs. Oh, and another thing, this ‘last experience’ is not the last.”

With that the man turned and walked back to join the groups of people still sitting, talking and laughing. Ros watched with longing as he walked away. One group of people had formed a circle and were singing together. It was an old song and Ros seemed to know some of the words. More than anything she wanted to join them too but she knew she had to continue. Apparently, there was more for her to see. The man turned and waved good-bye to her. Others joined in. Ros smiled and waved back before continuing along the path, the familiar song on her lips.

– Chapter 29 –

The sun was getting low in the sky when Ros came to an open area. There were a few trees with leaves that had already turned to scarlet, russet and gold. The ground was stony and uneven here, and she had to watch her step. Huge boulders blocked the path and she had to make her way around them. Dominating the scene, however, was the mountain, right in front of her, just a short distance ahead. It wasn't very big, more of a large hill, really, but its jagged features and stony outcrops suggested 'mountain'.

When she reached its base, the path seemed to stop. For a moment, Ros was confused. Was she meant to find her way around or climb over? She wasn't sure which would be quicker. Although it wasn't very high, it looked steep, with sharp edges and no discernible trail. She thought for a moment, considering what would happen if she fell, and decided to try going around.

As she walked, she noticed light glinting off some of the smaller stones that littered the ground. She stopped to pick one up and was amazed to see an array of colours dancing through it, black, blue and gold mostly, as she turned it in her hand. She knew nothing about geology but guessed that this might be some kind of semi-precious stone, or perhaps an ore. She put it down again and continued walking. Eventually she reached what she calculated to be the half-way mark, given that the sun had been in front of her when she arrived at the mountain and now it was behind her. This side looked the same as the other side and she wondered at her reason for being here. Walking a little further, she noticed an indentation. As she got closer, she realised it was the entrance to a cave. Reluctant, at first, to go in, and keeping a safe distance, she took a cautious look from the outside. There seemed to be no danger.

It took a while for her eyes to adjust to the dim interior but she walked further in, touching the rough, uneven walls as she went. The cave was a reasonable size, roughly the same as the reception area in the library, she reckoned. The walls were sharp in some places, but the floor was relatively smooth. Had others been here to wear it down? If the stones had value, the cave would surely have been mined yet there were no signs of mining activity; no tools or trolleys or other paraphernalia left behind. She discounted this notion.

As she pondered these things, the sun worked its way round to the mouth of the cave. When it reached the point where it was directly outside the cave's opening, rays of strong sunlight, like lasers, penetrated the doorway illuminating the cave completely. Ros gasped and covered her eyes. She had to turn and move to one side of the cave so she could see what was happening.

In front of her was a spectacle she had never seen, or expected to see, in her life. Dazzling crystals jutted from the sides and hung from the ceiling as stalactites. The sight took her breath away. She reached out and, lifting a large piece of quartz, held it in her hand, gradually turning it, allowing it to catch the light. As the sun struck the crystal, the light broke into a full spectrum of rainbow colours that poured out in all directions. Every stone that lined the walls, every sharp protrusion from floor to ceiling caught the colours and mirrored them, dazzling her. She had found treasure.

She turned her back and, shading the stone she was holding, looked more carefully at its shape. It was the size of her hand with a number of spiky formations along its length. She noticed a larger one on the edge which seemed to have a smaller protrusion coming directly from it rather than from the base. Ros considered this, then wondered why she found it so interesting. Somehow, it made her think of a parent and child and she thought of her mother. Was there another message here? There seemed to be one with everything else. Was she to give more of her time to her mother? Was she to take on the role of a parent and become responsible for her mother's care? Another thought came to mind. Perhaps she was neglecting her inner child, the part of her that saw wonder in everything; the part of her that wanted to play, to enjoy life. Closing her eyes, she held the crystal cupped in her hands for a moment. All of these thoughts seemed relevant but what did they all mean? After some thought she decided to take them all on board and follow whatever guidance came her way. Gently she returned the crystal to its place.

When she came out of the cave, the light was fading. She sat on a large stone just outside the doorway, letting thoughts come and go as they pleased. She wondered if her message might be of maturity, of taking responsibility not only for her mum but for herself and her own well-being. There was the thought of treasure but not physical treasure. Ros knew that the insights she found were her real treasure, but she needed to give them more consideration, allow them time to sink in and become part of her. Also, she couldn't shake the feeling that there was something more. Had she missed something?

Eventually, she became aware of the landscape changing. Grasses turned golden brown, flowers faded and plants drew back into the ground as they saved their energy for a new season.

She watched as leaves began to fall from the trees, first one then another, and another. Suddenly, the ground was littered with them until the wind blew, strong and cold, scattering them in all directions. Ros got the message. Smiling, she rose and started walking.

Ros followed the meandering path, walking slowly and gently, as if in a light trance. When she looked up, a smooth, clear blue lake, lined with evergreens, stood before her. The mountain she had just left was now somehow beyond the lake and topped with snow. It was an idyllic scene. All that seemed to be missing was a log cabin.

A fallen tree lay on the ground just off to her left and she took the opportunity to sit down, drinking in the beauty and the tranquillity of this place. It was good to rest. She felt serene and still, totally at peace. This setting lent itself to contemplation and she was grateful to have time to reflect. The day was nearly over. Would this be her last experience on the island? It seemed logical.

She thought about all she had encountered. She had understood what she needed to know from each. No one had told her, except when she met the others. It was true she had been given helpful information. Were these the 'helpful friends' James had spoken of? But she had also relied on her own feelings. When she thought about it, that wasn't entirely true. She had 'sensed' most of it, her imagination and intuition coming into full play. The challenges she had in her life seemed less threatening. She knew that everything was under control, that she had the ability to see things from a different perspective and the creativity to overcome obstacles. Things would happen as they were meant to happen and she wouldn't worry or try to control outcomes. She felt as if she had found a new aspect of her 'self', a part of her that had been hidden, dormant, just waiting for her to find again – her treasure. The feeling empowered her and brought a knowing smile to her face. She would keep this feeling. She knew this was how she was meant to be, this was the true Ros.

It was almost dark and she was getting very cold. She drew her coat closer around her and rubbed her arms. Had she been on the island for an entire day or an entire year? She wasn't sure, yet, apart from a berry, she hadn't eaten anything nor had she felt the need to. Now she felt that she should be tired but she wasn't. The rules must be different here.

Ros realised that it was getting late and must be time to get back to the boat but she wasn't sure how. Had she walked all the way around the island? Apart from the people she met in the park, she had seen no one. What about all the other passengers? They couldn't have just disappeared. She stood and began walking in the direction that felt right. Unworried and unhurried, she knew in her bones that she would find her way. She just knew.

– Chapter 30 –

Ros woke up in bed. She had lost track of what day it was and had to check her diary before she felt centred again. Grabbing her dream journal from its place in the drawer, she wrote, and wrote until there was nothing left to write. When she read it back, she was surprised at the level of detail she had been able to remember: sights, sounds, even feelings. She recalled that, travelling back on the boat, people had spoken to her. They had shared stories of what they had seen and done. Frustratingly, she couldn't remember anything that had been said, just that the conversations had taken place.

The little pier was waiting for them when they returned and Ros remembered walking back down through the village, past all the houses to the place where her dream always started, and stopped. It was at that point that she had woken up. It was different this time. She knew she wouldn't have the dream again.

Ros had a lot of thinking to do and was glad that this was one of her days off. She didn't want to be interrupted. Making herself a coffee and positioning cushions behind her on the sofa, she went through the dream again and again in her mind. She knew instinctively that everything she had seen and heard and learnt and felt was for her benefit. It was as if all of this had been absorbed into her being, downloaded into her body's computer, and would be there for her to use as and when she needed it, forever. Was this the new Ros or just the 'real' Ros? Either way, she was ready for whatever life would bring her way.

It suddenly occurred to her that she hadn't seen Suzanne for some time, not even at work. It was possible that they had just missed each other. That had happened before. It was also possible that she had been so consumed with her own life and all that was going on that days had simply melted into one another and slipped by unnoticed. She hadn't even looked for her friend. A pang of guilt went through her, and she vowed to phone in the afternoon. Suzanne would want to know that she'd had the dream again, and especially that she had been on the island. More than anything, Ros wanted to tell her.

Ros felt different as she went through her day. She thought again about how the dream seemed to have lasted a day, yet she felt as though she had been through a year, having experienced all the seasons. 'Dreams are funny like that,' she thought, calculating that she had only slept for seven hours.

Unable to wait till the afternoon, she phoned Suzanne late morning, wondering if she could fit in a coffee with her before going to see her mum. It was good to hear her friend's voice.

"It seems like ages since we spoke," Ros said.

"Yes, sorry I haven't been in touch but I've had a bit of a cold and took a few days off to stay at home."

"Sorry to hear that. I could phone back another time, if that's better."

"No, no. I'm fine now. How are you? And, more to the point, how is your mother?"

"I'm fine, thank you and Mum is doing really well. There's talk of her getting out soon."

"Oh, that sounds positive."

"Well, I don't know if she will get to come home or not.

There's this horrible woman who wants Mum to go into a care home. But I've got loads to tell you. Do you feel up to meeting for a coffee sometime?"

"Tomorrow would suit me best, if that's okay with you."

"Tomorrow's fine. I'll be working but could meet you about 12:00 at the little coffee shop. We could get a light lunch."

"Perfect. I'll see you then."

Although Ros was anxious to tell Suzanne about her dream, she would have to be patient. She convinced herself that it would give her time to go over everything again. All the aspects of her time on the island were still with her, nothing had faded. She remembered every detail, and it stirred her heart. It occurred to her that she didn't really need to discuss it at all with Suzanne, in terms of understanding. But she had been with Ros since the dream started and had helped her through the confusion. Suddenly now, everything was clear and Ros knew that she had exactly what she needed to face the Charge Nurse, the changes at work or any other challenge that came her way.

– *We do a great delivery service.*

Ros smiled as she remembered the lady in the shop telling her that. She now understood exactly what she had meant.

It was a joy to see Suzanne when they met the next day. Ros had made her way to the coffee shop a little earlier and found a table. Suzanne arrived a few minutes later and they smiled warmly as they hugged each other. Suzanne assured Ros that her cold was nothing to be concerned about and that she just needed a couple of days to rest and allow herself to heal. She was anxious to hear Ros' news.

"You've had the dream again, haven't you?"

Ros sat back in her chair and stared at her. "How do you do that?"

They both laughed.

Ros launched into her story. She had only intended giving Suzanne the highlights but Suzanne asked a million questions. She wanted to know everything.

"That sounds amazing," she said when Ros had finished.

"It was amazing. It was all so real."

"Do you remember the journey home?"

Ros thought that a strange question. "I do, actually." And here was something she hadn't mentioned. "The people on the boat talked to me as we sailed home. Not all of them, of course, but the ones who were nearby. We each talked of our experiences on the island."

"Were they the same as yours?"

"It might sound silly, but I don't remember what we said, exactly, just general impressions. I think some were similar, others completely different, at least, that's the feeling I have. Perhaps they had gone to a different part of the island or something."

"Maybe you don't need to keep that information."

Ros hadn't thought of that.

"You said you got 'messages'," Suzanne continued, unperturbed.

"I did. It sounds a bit strange talking about it now but it seemed like every place I visited, every experience I had, told me something. I know that sounds weird but honestly, it was all so clear, so distinct."

"And were these messages helpful?"

"Oh, yes. They were all about trusting myself and my own intuition; about being balanced and taking things in my stride, being flexible in my approach but not letting anyone throw me off."

"Hmm. Very helpful, I would say, given your current situation. Quite relevant, really."

"I suppose you're right." Ros said thoughtfully.

"Of course, helpful for other situations as well, and good life skills generally."

"I think it was what I needed to hear, to know, right now. I was struggling." Ros dropped her gaze and thought for a moment before continuing. "I think I'd lost my way recently and this has helped me find it again."

"I didn't know you before. Would you say you're back to being your old self?"

Ros gave a little frown as she thought about this. Suzanne had a knack of reaching right into her soul and asking piercing questions. It often brought difficult memories to the surface, forcing Ros to face the things she'd hidden away. But Ros knew she always felt better for it.

She thought about her life before her split with Matthew. It was true she had been more sociable, much more. She'd had friends and they went out together to events or even just a shopping trip. She was astute and quick thinking, and was able to anticipate little things that could be done, at work or at home, to make life easier for herself and others. She had accepted people as they were, was outgoing and cheerful. Since then, everything had changed, everything seemed a chore, an imposition; even her mum at times. She loved her mother, of course, but going up to the hospital every day, dealing with changes at work, trying to cook, eat, do laundry... it seemed relentless, and a bit overwhelming at times. There were times when she thought that running away and hiding, not seeing anyone or doing anything, would have suited her very well.

Suzanne was looking at her. "I'd locked myself away, when

Matthew and I split up." Ros couldn't disguise the sadness in her voice. Suzanne reached out and touched her arm reassuringly. "I guess I was afraid, afraid of being hurt again."

"You were trying to protect yourself."

"Yes. Yes, that's it exactly. But how could I let one person do all that to me?"

"It's understandable, given the circumstances."

"But look what it's done. I've effectively lost two years of my life. I could have had friends, I could even have found someone else, been happy, but I didn't even try."

"Maybe you needed that time to heal. Maybe you're ready now to be happy again. Maybe that's what you dream has been trying to tell you. And it sounds to me like you got the message."

Ros tried not to cry. She wasn't angry or upset. It was a release. She pictured the leaves falling from the trees in her dream and immediately saw the connection. It was time to let go.

– Chapter 31 –

The weekend passed, as it normally did, but Ros was upbeat. She was armed and ready for the meeting having arranged to take next Friday off work. She wanted nothing to interfere with this. Her mother had to be discharged to her own house. Nothing else was acceptable. She wanted to be there now, this minute, to get this problem settled. But this was only Monday and she would have to wait.

Ros came back from her break to find a small crowd of excited, noisy people gathered close to her desk. They were all members of staff but they were so crammed together that Ros couldn't see what was going on. She suddenly saw Eleanor who turned and saw her at the same time.

"Oh, Ros. Over here, you have to come and see."

Puzzled, she went over and, as people separated to let her in, she saw what all the fuss was about.

"Kath!" she cried. "What a surprise!" It was good to see her colleague. It was also good to see the little girl she was holding. "You look wonderful."

"You look different," Kath said, leaning back slightly and studying her. "I love the hair style. It really suits you."

"Well, it was time for a change. I didn't know you were coming in today."

"No one did, except Eleanor. I gave her a call so she could be here as well. I just got here, actually."

Ros looked at the tiny bundle in Kath's arms and it warmed her heart. "Can I hold her?"

There were shouts of 'me too' and 'wait your turn' from some of the others. But it was decided that, as Ros worked on Reception, and was likely to be busy, she could go first. Kath promised to come round to all the sections before she left.

As she opened the blanket and removed the delicate, pink crocheted hat, Ros gasped. A tiny round face with big brown eyes looked back at her, the little head covered with a mass of thick, dark hair. Ros stared in disbelief. This little one looked exactly as Kath had described her before going off on maternity leave. But Ros was beginning to believe in dreams and visions. She looked at Kath and gave her a knowing smile. "What's her name? How old is she now?"

"Her name is Faith, after my grandmother and she is two weeks old."

Kath went through all the details – the date she was born, birth weight, the ambulance ride, length of labour, everything. Ros listened but didn't really take it all in. There was something magical about holding a new baby, something that brought out the best in people. Perhaps it brought people back to their own childhood. She looked at this little being, this new life and thought of new beginnings and happy times ahead. Everyone had to have a turn holding the baby. Some went back to their sections and Kath started to make her rounds.

Eleanor took a moment to come and speak with Ros. "I see Karen got my post," she said.

"Yes. I was hoping it would be someone else, maybe from one of the branches, but, it is what it is."

"I know she can be difficult. I feel a bit guilty, actually."

"Guilty? For what?"

"Leaving."

"Eleanor, don't be silly. You were here a long time and you should relax and enjoy your retirement. You had nothing to do with Karen getting the job."

"I know, but I feel bad about it."

"You've always cared about the people you worked with, everybody here knows that. We'll be fine with Karen, don't worry."

Eleanor visibly relaxed.

"Besides," Ros added, "I'm very good at avoiding her."

They both laughed. Eleanor stayed a few minutes longer and the two women chatted and caught up with each other's news. When she left, Ros felt a tinge of sadness.

The rest of the day passed quickly and was largely uneventful. Ros decided to call into her flat and retrieve any mail, as well as doing a few domestic jobs to make sure the place was in order. The first thing she did when she got there was open the windows. She looked around but there was really nothing else that needed to be done. Her flat suddenly seemed small and cramped. She had been here a long time, twelve years, by her calculation. She had shared it with Matthew when they were together. Most of that time had been happy, until she found out what he was up to. After the split, it had become her retreat. It had obviously suited her at the time, met her needs. Now she saw it with different eyes. She had wanted to be small, confined, limited. Now it felt stifling. She had changed. Perhaps she should look for a bigger flat, maybe in the spring.

There was more to do at her mum's house. Ros got some clean clothes to take to the hospital. She had something to eat and, taking some chocolate biscuits from the kitchen cupboard, made her way out the door. She arrived to find her mother in an anxious mood.

"Roslyn, take me home, please!" she shouted.

"Mum, what's wrong?"

"I can't take another day in this place. It's nothing but questions and endless tests and people keep telling me what I can and can't do. I want to go home. I want to go home now."

Her mother started to cry. Ros frowned, wondering how long she had been feeling like this and saying nothing.

"Mum," she said gently holding her face between her hands and looking into her eyes. "I love you. You know I would take you home right now this very minute, if I could but it would be better if the doctor said it was all right first. I want you to come home, Mum, but I need to know you're well so I can care for you properly."

She put her arms around her mother and held her close, letting her mum's head rest against her chest. Her mother stopped crying and her body softened. Ros wasn't sure if it was exasperation, resignation or just fatigue, but she held her mother and kissed her gently on the top of her head. Ros told her about the meeting she was going to in a few days. She said that a decision would be made then about when she would be able to leave hospital. Ros watched as her mother's eyes widened and she sat up straight.

"Just a few more days, Mum; a few more days and we'll know what's happening. Okay?"

Satisfied, her mother nodded and relaxed back against the pillows on her bed.

Ros tried to keep the conversation light and told her mother about Kath bringing her new baby into work. Her mother clearly enjoyed hearing this and began talking about Ros when she was a baby and how she hardly had any hair at all until she was one, but then, she hadn't suffered from heartburn during her pregnancy. Apparently that was a sign of 'lots of hair' on a newborn baby.

On the way back to her mother's house, Ros thought about her flat and her job. She loved staying at her mum's but she knew that was only temporary. She could get a bigger flat and began to wonder what price her flat would sell for. She thought of where the new flat might be to be convenient for her mum and work. Did she even want a flat? She would have no garden. She wondered why that was suddenly important.

– Chapter 32 –

Friday morning arrived. Putting on her new blouse and sweater, Ros readied herself for the day ahead. She felt remarkably calm, given the uncertainty of what the outcome of the meeting might be. She arrived early to make sure she was in the right place. Dr Thomson was already there and welcomed her. She relaxed knowing that he, at least, would be willing to listen to what she had to say.

As the others arrived and took their places, Ros listened to the chat and got the feeling that most members of the group were open-minded, all except Charge Nurse Fraser. She glared at Ros, annoyed, no doubt, that she was there. Ros listened carefully to what each person had to say. She knew many of the points they made were valid and she took them on board, making notes as she went along. When Charge Nurse Fraser spoke, Ros remained calm and listened.

"Mrs Malcolm is a lovely lady, I'm sure, but her behaviour has been challenging at times."

People lifted their heads and frowned slightly. Ros said nothing.

"She has been aggressive and disruptive, even throwing a plate of food on the floor in a fit of temper. It would be reckless to send her home to her own house. What if she injured herself and no one was there? She needs constant care from people who are trained, and equipped, to deal with her illness and the fluctuations in temperament."

Charge Nurse Fraser went on to relate specific details with dates and times of incidents where staff had to calm her mother down and help her back into bed, or calm another patient who became upset at what was going on.

People asked questions and took notes, taking everything into account. They talked amongst themselves and put their own perspectives forward. One suggested that a care package could be put together to allow her mum to be at home but with added support. This sounded just what Ros, and her mother, were looking for.

Someone else said that her condition would get worse and that wouldn't be fair on her daughter, as if Ros wasn't in the room. The physiotherapist seemed to have no problem with her and said she was a 'delightful lady'. There were a lot of different opinions but no consensus.

"May I say something?" Ros spoke above the din. A hush fell on the room.

"Of course, Miss Malcolm. We realise you have responsibility for your mother and we would be interested to hear your thoughts."

Charge Nurse Fraser glared.

"I was not aware of all the issues that have been spoken about today. Perhaps if I had been informed at the time, we would be having a different conversation. The point is, I know my mother. The behaviour you mention is totally out of character for her. I believe she is frustrated at being kept in hospital for so long, longer than she expected to be, and she would take that frustration with her to another medical setting, regardless of how good a care facility it might be. Having to go through all the tests and assessments and treatments have tired her out. Also, she's not used to taking so much medication and it seems that no one is telling her what's happening. She has been moved to a different room, with no one else to talk to and has been feeling disoriented and lonely. When she is returned to her own home, with familiar things around her, she will be more secure and relaxed."

People talked again, nodding and making more notes.

"But she needs someone there with her all the time," Charge Nurse Fraser said.

"I will be with her."

"But you work, part-time I know, but there will be times when you won't be there. She needs someone all the time, as I said."

Dr Thomson spoke up. "Perhaps the care package we talked about earlier could be put in place."

The Social Worker joined in. "We could provide extra support for the days Miss Malcolm is working."

They talked again amongst themselves and spoke of various departmental issues that Ros knew nothing about. All she knew was that things seemed to be going her way.

The Social Worker spoke directly to Ros. "This will be hard work, Miss Malcolm. Are you sure this is what you want?"

"Absolutely. My mother looked after me for long enough, now it's my turn to care for her." Ros smiled and the Social Worker smiled too. "Then I suggest we discharge Mrs Malcolm to her own home with extra support as discussed. The situation will be reviewed regularly to identify any changes in Mrs Malcolm's condition and care requirements."

It was agreed. Ros was delighted, yet, somehow, not surprised. This was the outcome she had anticipated.

The meeting ended. As they left, Charge Nurse Fraser brought her face close to Ros and said in a low, intense voice, "You don't know what you're taking on."

Ros returned her stare saying, "Oh, I think I do."

The treatments and tests had been completed, just paperwork to be finished, then prescriptions to get ready and the extra care arrangements made. A date was set for her mother's discharge the following week. Ros would be bringing her mother home on Wednesday. She couldn't wait.

Ros knew she had made a big commitment during the meeting but regretted nothing. She also knew that her mother's condition would change as time went on but she didn't know what those changes might be, or the timescale involved. It would be better to spend this time with her mum while she could and to be there to help her through those changes.

Ros was rather pleased with herself. She had faced the dragon, and won. She didn't feel any sense of victory though. The decision that was made was the right one. The way she saw it, it was the only one that made sense. But she had put her case across in a logical, balance and unflustered way. People had listened to her and acknowledged what she had to say. There had been no tension, no anxiety on her part, just a calm acceptance of what was happening. It was as if she only had to put her point across then sit back and let events unfold naturally, organically; as if the words she said, and the way she said them, had the power to make the required changes. She had never felt that way before. She liked this new Ros.

Although Ros knew that Dr Thomson would let her mother know how the meeting went and the decisions that were made, she would see her in the afternoon and they could make plans. She headed for the cafe, anxious for it to be visiting time.

– Chapter 33 –

Wednesday finally arrived. Ros went to the hospital at eleven o'clock, as arranged, to bring her mother home.

"Your mother's ready for you," the young nurse chirped. "She's waiting in the patients' lounge at the far end of the ward." The nurse started walking and Ros followed. "She's a lovely lady, your mum, and she's so excited about getting home. She's done really well while she was here. Physio and O T, sorry, Occupational Therapy, are very happy with her."

Ros would have responded if she could have got a word in. Still, she was happy to hear her mum being spoken of so positively. She remembered considering nursing as a career when she was younger. Why hadn't she done that?

"Here you are," the nurse said opening the door to the lounge and turning towards Ros' mum. "If you just wait here for a few minutes, Mrs Malcolm I'll see if the pharmacy has your prescription ready."

Mother and daughter hugged, excitement and relief evident on her mum's face and in the intensity of their embrace. Although Ros had taken most of her mother's clothes home already, she'd had the foresight to bring a small suitcase for her overnight things and began to put slippers, wash bag and other odds and ends inside. After a few minutes, the nurse appeared with medications and instructions for their use, as well as a bag of laundry for them to take with them. That filled the tiny case and, as her mother had to use a walking frame, Ros was glad the case had wheels. They were able to walk at a suitable pace with nothing to carry. When they got to the car, Ros helped her mum in and made sure she was comfortable. It was clear that she still had some pain in her hip.

"Would you like to go somewhere for lunch, Mum?" she asked, pulling on her seatbelt and inserting the key in the ignition. "It's been a long time since we did that."

"I'd rather just go home, if you don't mind."

"No problem. We can do that another day."

It wasn't a long drive to the house. Ros had to help her mum out of the car and up to the front door. She opened the door and saw her mum safely inside. The house was all on one level so she was able to use her walking frame to go wherever she wanted to go. She headed straight for her bedroom. Ros went back to the car and began bringing in her mother's belongings. She put everything down in the hallway and went to check on the meal she had started earlier in the slow cooker. It was progressing nicely but wouldn't be ready until early evening so she put the kettle on and began making sandwiches.

"Do you want a cup of tea, Mum?" she called from the kitchen.

It was only when she didn't get a reply that she walked along the hall to her mother's room and saw her.

"Oh, Mum. What's wrong?" She sat on the bed beside her tearful mother. "I thought you'd be happy to be home."

"Oh, I am, Darling," her mum sniffed.

"Then, what's bothering you?"

"This," she said, looking around the room and opening her hands out in front of her. "I was beginning to think I would never see it again."

Ros was silent for a moment then, handing her mum a tissue said, "Come on, I need your opinion."

Her mother was perplexed but stood up, still dabbing at her eyes. Allowing Ros to help her, she walked slowly into the sitting room. Her face lit up when she saw what Ros had done. There was bunting along the curtain rail at the front window saying 'Welcome Home Mum' and a huge bouquet of flowers on the little table in the corner.

"I wasn't sure whether to get pink flowers or yellow, so I got a mixture. I hope that's all right."

"They're beautiful, Ros, just beautiful. All of this is lovely."

Ros helped her mum to her favourite chair and watched the expression of familiar satisfaction as she sat in it. She brought her a tray with tea, a sandwich and some of the fruit cake she knew her mother liked and hadn't had for some time

"I feel like I've been away for ages," her mother said. "I suppose it's only been a few weeks."

"It's been four weeks, Mum. You've been through a lot," Ros said. "So much has happened."

"For you as well as me," her mum said.

Ros was confused for a moment. "Oh, my hair. Yes, I suppose so."

"Your clothes too. You suit brighter colours."

"Thanks, Mum. You're right, a lot has changed."

Ros considered their situation. This was the day she had waited for, the day her mother had waited for. She wondered where they would go from here. A feeling gripped her, a feeling of uncertainty, a feeling that there was more to come. She would face that when she had to. For now, her mother was happy and that was what she wanted to focus on. "Mum, you know I've taken some time off work."

Her mum had just taken a mouthful of cake and simply nodded before being able to say, "Yes, I remember you saying that."

"Well, I'm off this Friday and all of next week, so if there's anywhere you want to go or anything you would like to do, or want me to do, just tell me. Okay?"

She took a sip of tea before saying, "I'm happy just to take things easy for a while."

"See how you feel in a day or two. There's no rush."

"Ros."

"Yes, Mum?"

"I'm glad you're here."

Life settled down nicely over the next few days. Ros had made a list of her mum's medication and when each had to be taken. She did the cooking but her mother liked to do little jobs around the house too. She was still in some pain and limited by having to use the walking frame but she knew the importance of keeping mobile. Ros caught her once or twice trying to walk without it and they had a discussion about what would happen if she fell again. Ros reminded her that she had the frame because she needed it and, until the doctor told her anything different, she should continue to use it. She felt a bit odd talking to her mother like that; as if she was the parent and her mum was the child. She thought again of the quartz crystal she had held in her dream.

Letters started arriving, almost daily, and suddenly her mum had appointments to keep. There had been an issue with her hearing and she had to attend the clinic to have a hearing test. She also had to get new glasses and attend a physiotherapy session at the hospital where they tried to get her walking with a stick rather than the walker. She was still a little unsteady so another appointment was made for a few weeks later. She had to attend an out-patient clinic for the rash on her face, although, as it turned out, no treatment was needed other than an antiseptic cream.

A Mrs Jenkins from Social Work Department arranged to come to the house to discuss a care package. The discussion lasted for some time and was quite in-depth. Ros and her mum answered all Mrs Jenkins' questions and were able to ask a few of their own. It became obvious that Mrs Jenkins had encountered similar concerns from other clients and was able to reassure them. In the end, it was decided that two carers would come in twice a day to help her mum get up in the morning and go to bed at night. They would also call in at midday on the days that Ros was at work to ensure that her mum had taken her medication and had something to eat.

There was something else too, something neither Ros, nor her mother, had thought about. A place was available at a local Day Centre. It was only one day a week but it meant that her mum could be with people her own age and with similar interests. Ros was delighted. Her mum said she would have to think about it. Ros knew that her mum had been lonely for some time and was surprised at her hesitation. On reflection, she wondered if her mum needed some time to settle at home first.

Ros was glad she had taken some of her holiday leave but the time went quickly. She didn't want to go back to work. She knew Karen was now Supervisor and she dreaded it. She had done her best to have as little to do with Karen as possible. That had been relatively easy as they worked in different sections but this new appointment altered everything. Karen would make changes, she expected that, but there would be no consultation, no opportunity for people to exchange ideas or express concerns, not like when Eleanor was there. Still, there was no point worrying about it. She would simply have to deal with the new regime, whatever that happened to be. But when Monday morning came, she walked into a very different workplace to the one she had left.

– Chapter 34 –

Ros went straight to her desk. She put her bag on the floor underneath and was about to sit down when she saw Karen approach.

"Ah, Ros, I hope you had a good holiday."

"It wasn't a holiday, Karen. My mum got out of hospital."

"Oh, good. Well, as your new Supervisor," she said with a sway of her head, "I wanted to say hi to you personally since you weren't here last week when I spoke with everyone."

"Karen, we know each other."

"Yes, and I know we've had our differences, but we're both mature, intelligent adults and I'm sure we can put all that behind us." She smiled insincerely. "Exciting things are happening, Ros. I would really like you to be part of this."

"Part of what, Karen?"

"All the changes."

Ros sighed heavily. "What changes, Karen?"

"Well, one thing at a time. There are plans to upgrade the computer system and install more computers for the public to use."

Ros shrugged. "No problem. I can be part of that."

"There are a few other things in the pipeline as well but they're still at the planning stage so I can't say too much just now." Karen looked pleased with herself, a look that worried Ros but she wasn't going to let it show.

"Okay."

Karen's expression changed to one of annoyance. "Aren't you going to ask what they are?"

"I'm sure I'll find out in the course of time. Nice talking to you, Karen, but right now, I'm going to get a coffee and start work."

"No coffee at the desk, Ros."

"What?"

"You'll have to wait for your break, I'm afraid."

Ros looked around as Karen walked away. It was still early. There was no one about. Having a quick cup of coffee had never been a problem when Eleanor was there, as long as it didn't interfere with work. Sadly, Eleanor wasn't there and Karen was being pedantic. 'Still,' Ros thought, through gritted teeth, 'I am a 'mature, intelligent adult'. It's only a little over an hour till break time. I can wait.'

Picking up the papers from her tray, she began sorting through them and putting them into neat piles. She reached for her stapler but it wasn't in the drawer. She looked to the raised shelf on the desk, the one with all the little cubby-holes at the back that held the stationery items she used most in the course of a day. It wasn't there. She looked in surprise and disbelief. The whole unit was gone. Why hadn't she noticed that when she came in? Checking the drawers and cupboards underneath the desk, she realised that almost everything had been moved; nothing was in the right place.

Since she and Jennifer job-shared, Ros assumed that Jennifer would have covered for her while she was off. But they knew each other's routine. She wouldn't have totally reorganised the desk. Even if Jennifer couldn't come in for the whole week, there was no one she knew of who would totally change someone else's workspace.

Ros was angry and flustered. By the time she had re-organised her desk the way she needed it to be, she was more than ready for her break and made her way to the staff room.

"I saw Karen talking to you this morning."

Ros stopped stirring her coffee and turned to see who was talking to her.

"Jennifer? This is Monday. I didn't expect to see you today."

"Derek's off sick and I was asked to come in and cover for him."

"Oh. Is he all right?"

"Stress. He's off for two weeks."

"Stress? Derek?"

"I know. I've never seen anyone more laid-back. Anyway, it's good to see you. It's only been a week but Karen's making her mark. What did she tell you?"

"Very little. But now I know why I stayed out of her way. There are very few people I don't get on with, but she has a way of drip-feeding information that really gets to me. You have to ask question after question to get the whole story, and she just stands there smirking at you as if she has the power to decide whether to tell you or not."

Jennifer raised her eyebrows. "Ros, I've never seen you so het up."

Ros took a deep breath. "Sorry. I shouldn't let her do that to me. How are you, anyway? We never get to speak to each other."

"I know. I'm okay, thanks. But I think we're all a bit concerned about these new changes Karen is hinting at. She got everyone together last week to 'introduce' herself, like we don't know her already. She talked for an hour and said nothing. I just wondered if she'd told you anything new."

"She said we're upgrading the computer system. That's no

problem. There were a few other things she didn't go into detail about and I wasn't going to ask her. Something about changes coming and she hoped I would 'be part of it.'"

"That's a bit cryptic," Jennifer frowned. "What did you say?"

"Well, I can hardly work here not be part of whatever changes are going on. Why? What is going on?"

"Nobody knows. She's not saying anything specific just dropping little seeds then drawing back. You know what she's like. To be honest, we're starting to worry about our jobs."

Ros hadn't expected to hear this. She thought for a moment. "I don't think she could do anything to our jobs. Changes like that would have to be approved by the council."

"I know, but she's got everybody on edge. It's like she's got this little secret going on in her head and one day, when she's ready, she's just going to spring it on us." Jennifer got up and washed her cup.

"Jennifer, were you on Reception last week?"

"No. I was put into General Lending. Why?"

"The desk was totally disorganised. I didn't think it was you."

"Someone else was on Reception. I don't know his name, but he hasn't been here very long, only a few months. I think he works in the Children's bit." Jennifer's face darkened. "See what I mean about our jobs? Be careful, Ros."

Ros was glad to see the end of the day. This was the first time her mum had been on her own since she came out of hospital and Ros was anxious to make sure she was all right. It was as she was tidying her desk for the evening that Karen came up to speak to her.

"The upgrade I told you about will be starting in a few weeks, Ros. Just thought I'd let you know. You'll get a memo in the morning."

"Okay," Ros said, unperturbed.

"There will have to be some staff training beforehand, of course. There's a meeting on Thursday to let everyone know how that will work."

"I'm not in on Thursday, Karen. You know that. I'll catch up on Friday."

"No. I'm afraid everyone has to be here."

Ros stopped what she was doing and put her hands on the desk. "Two things: firstly, I don't work on Thursdays; and second, I care for my mother. I can't just leave her."

"You'll get paid."

"It's not about being paid. It's about the time involved."

"You need to be here, Ros. Make whatever arrangements you need to for your mother. The meeting starts at nine o'clock, sharp."

– Chapter 35 –

Ros had no intention of going in to work on Thursday morning. As it turned out, she had to go to the medical centre to pick up a prescription and her mother decided to go with her. Although Ros was concerned about all the medication that her mum had to take, it was clearly helping her and she was almost back to being her normal self. They went to the supermarket for the shopping, the way they used to, but stopped at the cafe first for something to eat.

"We haven't done this for a while," Ros said as she helped her mum onto the chair.

"Yes. This is nice. I'd almost forgotten what it was like."

Ros watched as her mum ate her soup and noticed that her right hand was shaking.

"Hold on, Mum. I'll be back in a minute."

Confused, her mother watched as Ros made her way to the till. She spoke to the attendant and returned with two mugs. Pouring both her soup and her mother's into the mugs, she sat down again and watched as her mum picked the mug up with both hands and drank the warm liquid easily.

"That was a good idea," she smiled and took another sip.

Ros was lost in thought, wondering if she should mention the shaking hand to the doctor, when she heard her mother speaking.

"I've been thinking, Ros," she began, then stopped as if

uncertain of how to proceed.

"Are you okay, Mum?"

"Yes, yes, I'm fine, Darling."

She stopped again, thinking.

"So, what have you been thinking about?"

She looked up and Ros thought she could see sadness in her eyes.

"Ros, I don't want you to be upset," she began. Ros was immediately upset. "I know I'm not going to get better."

"What are you talking about? You're much better now than when you first went into hospital."

"Yes, and I'm grateful for that but I know I won't ever be myself again. I won't be able to do the things I used to do, looking after the house, cooking, things like that."

"But I'm here with you, Mum. You don't have to do all those things yourself."

"I don't know what I would do without you, to be honest. But you have your own house and your own life. I've been wondering how I will cope when you go home again."

"I'll stay with you for as long as you need me, Mum. You'll be ready to throw me out in a month or two." Ros' attempt at humour fell flat.

"I don't want you to leave, Ros. I love having you with me. I love the company, as well as the help you give me. I just can't help wondering if you're happy being with me?"

"I love being with you, Mum. I see you every day and I know you're keeping well, eating properly, getting to appointments, all of that. That puts my mind at ease. And to be honest, I love being in the house again."

Ros saw her mother's shoulders relax. "What's on your mind, Mum? You can tell me."

"I would love you to stay with me, Ros. I don't want to be alone again."

Ros pressed her lips together and was quiet for a moment. This was unexpected. Thoughts raced through her mind. She knew she had to be still, to calm the chatter. She needed to put all these ideas together, consider different options. But for now, she needed to reassure her mother.

"I would love to stay with you, Mum, but it's a big change and I have some things to consider."

Her mother dropped her head and nodded.

"Give me a little time to think about this and I'll come up with something that will work for both of us. Is that okay?"

Her mum raised her head and smiled. "Yes," she said. "Yes that's okay,"

When she did think about it, Ros was delighted by her mum's request. It opened up a lot of new avenues for her, gave her opportunities she hadn't considered, but she had to think about how it would all work.

If she was to move in with her mum permanently, it would make sense to sell her flat. Perhaps she could look into that with her solicitor, make some preliminary inquiries. There were also legal implications to consider. She knew her mother owned her home outright, but if her mum did end up going into care, might the house have to be sold? That was something else she would have to ask about. Ros' job was only part time and the salary wasn't very big. However, with no mortgage to pay, it would be enough to let her share the costs of running the house. She had some savings and with the money she would make from the sale of her flat, she could keep that money aside for a deposit on another house, if she needed it. She could see this working out well for both of them and the thought excited her.

Ros took a few days to go over everything in her mind. She could have done without going into work on Friday – Friday the thirteenth, she realised – and dismissed Karen's anger at her 'failure' to attend the meeting. She pointed out that her contract stipulated Monday, Tuesday and Friday as her working days. Also, she had the minutes of the meeting so was as up-to-date as everyone else with what was happening. Karen was furious. Ros didn't care.

On Sunday, Ros made a nice meal for her and her mum and they discussed their plans. Her mother was as excited by the idea as Ros had been. Although she insisted that she didn't want any money from Ros for the bills, Ros insisted she had to pay her way, so an agreement was struck. Ros would pay her mum a fixed cash sum every month as a contribution. Ros thought the sum too low but her mother was content with the arrangement.

Ros contacted her solicitor on Monday morning to put her flat on the market and was surprised at the price he thought she would get. He also thought it would sell quickly. It was in a nice area, in good condition and had been well maintained. He arranged to get someone up to take photographs on Wednesday. Things were falling into place nicely.

It was starting to get chilly and her mother seemed reluctant to turn the heating up. Ros reminded her that she would help with costs and that it was important for her to keep warm. She busied herself around the house, her home now as much as her mother's. It could do with a bit of upgrading and some decorating and maintenance here and there, but there was nothing that needed to be done immediately. She particularly enjoyed working in the garden and, had bought some autumn bedding plants to give colour to the front borders. She knew nothing of gardening but wanted to get the flowers into the ground before it got too cold.

"Good morning."

Ros looked up to see Mr Fielding walking up the street.

"You're doing a great job," he called from the path.

"Good morning, Mr Fielding," she stopped, knowing he would correct her. "Gregory." He smiled. "It's hard work but this should do it for the winter."

She walked down the path to talk to him without shouting. "I knew you lived close by but I wasn't sure where exactly. Mum said you helped with the gardening but I didn't like the idea of you coming a long way."

"No, don't worry about that. I live just there."

Ros looked where he was pointing. It seemed to be a house on the other side of the street and further down near the junction. "The one with the blue door?"

"That's right, so not far at all really."

"Oh, that's not so bad," Ros said.

"I'm still happy to help out, if you need me."

"Were you a gardener before you retired?"

"I worked with the council, Parks Department. I was there for thirty years and I loved every minute."

Ros spent some time talking to Gregory. She found that he grew fruit and vegetables in his own garden and he offered to help her set up a small kitchen garden in the spring. Ros was delighted. She was beginning to think about how badly she had thought of this man at the start. Yet here he was now, offering to help and that help was offered freely and without condition. Things certainly were changing. She was just ending the conversation by thanking him, when she saw the man walk up the street again, the same man she had seen before, the one at the hospital; she was sure it was him. He walked with his head down, paying no attention to anyone or anything around him. Mr Fielding saw her stare and turned to see what she was looking at. To Ros' amazement he shouted over to the man who stopped walking and turned to look at him. He then waved and came over to join them.

"Ros," Mr Fielding said, and he smiled while he spoke. "This is Alex, my son."

– Chapter 36 –

Ros was astounded. She carried on with her work, pretending not to watch them as they made their way to the end of the street and turned the corner. She wasn't sure what had just happened. She had smiled at Alex when his father had introduced them but he had barely responded. Maybe he didn't like her. She gave herself a shake. What difference did it make?

But she was confused and a little angry. Why would she feel an attraction the very first time she saw him, and then find that he lived close by and was related to a friend of her mother, only to find that he didn't like her. It seemed such a waste of time and energy. It seemed unfair too. Here she was, ready to begin a new life, open to new experiences and opportunities only to find the door slammed in her face. The digging tempered her frustration but she couldn't shake the feeling that something wasn't right. Maybe it had just been a bad time for him. Maybe he was upset or worried about something. It probably had nothing to do with her. Still, she couldn't be sure. If she talked to him again, and that seemed likely since his father lived across the street, she would be polite but distant and see how he reacted. She scolded herself for even thinking so much about it and carried on with her planting.

Having accepted the place offered to her in a local Day Centre, Ros' mum found that she really enjoyed it.

"We get tea or coffee with biscuits in the morning and the

afternoon, and we get a cooked meal at lunch time. The food's lovely," her mother raved.

"What about the people, Mum? Have you made any new friends?"

"Oh, the people are lovely too. Some of them are a bit elderly, poor souls, but they're very friendly and some have even been in hospital, just like me."

Seeing her mother so animated made Ros smile.

"You know," her mother continued, "sometimes they have events there; sing-songs and quizzes and such. They even go out for little trips in the minibus, although I think that depends on the weather."

"So you're going back again?" Ros asked.

"Of course I'm going back again. Oh, you don't mind do you, Dear?"

"No, Mum. I don't mind at all."

As her mother's allocated day was Wednesday, it meant that Ros would be able to see her onto the minibus in the morning and be there to welcome her home when she was dropped off in the afternoon. It also meant that Ros had a day to herself and she began to wonder what she might do with it. She thought again about taking up a hobby.

Ros had mentioned meeting Mr Fielding's son to see what her mother's reaction would be. She merely said, "Oh, yes. I knew he had a son. He drove him up to the hospital when he came to visit."

That explained why he was in the waiting room when she had first seen him. Although Ros tried to continue the conversation, it became clear that was all her mother knew of him. She let the matter drop and continued doing whatever needed to be done to make the house and garden ready for winter.

In the two weeks since meeting him, she saw Alex three times. Once when he was walking up to his dad's house and on that occasion, he waved as he walked by. Ros waved back. The second time, he stopped to say hello, crossing the street to talk with her for a few minutes. Ros decided she liked his company. On the third occasion he asked her out, just for coffee, some morning when she was free. She was happy with that. It was the first time she had seen him smile. She said Wednesday would suit her best.

Ros was ready early. It was a lovely day, bright and sunny with a slight chill in the air. The minibus came for her mum just after nine o'clock and Ros was meeting Alex at 10:30. She watched for him from the front window and as he walked up the street and onto her path, she waved at him and went to the door, noticing he hadn't brought a car.

"I hope you don't mind," Alex began, "I thought we could just walk down to the main street. There's a little place I know and I think you would like it."

Ros was intrigued. "Sounds interesting," she smiled. "Is the coffee good?"

"Best in town," Alex replied.

They chatted easily as they made their way along the streets, taking the odd short cut along dirt paths between the houses until the main thoroughfare was before them. They didn't have to walk far before they came to the place Alex had in mind.

"Here it is," he said opening the door for her.

Ros was confused. "But it's a book shop."

"Yes. And they do serve the best coffee in town. I wouldn't lie to you about a thing like that." He placed his hand on his heart and his eyes widened. He had the look of a little boy who had chocolate on his face but insisted he hadn't stolen a chocolate biscuit. Ros just laughed. She took a closer look at the front window which held a seasonal display. It was well laid out, full of colour and designed to suit a variety of interests and age ranges.

As they went in, the young girl behind the counter seemed to know Alex. He introduced her as 'Steph, my lovely assistant'. Ros thought it an odd thing to say but decided he might be a regular and this young woman had helped him find books he had been looking for. It was certainly an interesting shop. It wasn't very big but shelves along the back wall held a generous selection of books with winter themes – new titles and old favourites. There were posters and notices on the wall promoting local authors, advising customers of events such as book signings and new book groups starting up. There where stairs on the left leading to an upper floor. On one side of the staircase a narrow bookcase stood, beautifully decorated with gift ideas. On the other side was the serving counter which held a small but very interesting assortment of cakes and behind it, an impressive coffee machine. They sat at one of the small tables near the front window to have their coffee and a slice of homemade carrot cake.

"I've never noticed this place before," Ros said, looking round and taking in the decor. She stopped to read one of the quotes written on the wall: *Books; who says money can't buy happiness?*

"It's new," Alex was saying. "Just opened a few months ago."

"I guess I'm usually in the town. Maybe I'm missing out on the local shops. How did you find it?"

Alex looked a little sheepish. "Well, actually, it's mine."

"What?"

"It's my shop."

Ros stared at him. They looked at each other without talking for a moment before Alex said, "We're still working on it, got loads to do. There are lots of books upstairs. Would you like to have a look?"

"Yes." Her response was automatic. "Sorry, I'm still trying to get over the fact that this is actually your shop. It's fantastic. And yes, I would love to see upstairs."

Alex smiled the broadest smile Ros had seen from him so far. She couldn't help but smile back before following him to the upper floor. He talked all the way.

"Like I said, we still have lots to do, and so many ideas for displays and promotions and everything. It's going to be trial and error for a while – you know, see what works and what doesn't. We're really looking forward to it though, hard work, but worth it, hopefully."

"'The Book Keeper'. Where did you get that name?"

"From my accountant," Alex replied. Ros wasn't sure if he was joking or not.

Ros browsed the rows of books with interest, but something was niggling at her and she had to find out. She tried to word the question carefully. "You keep saying 'we' when you talk about the shop. Is there someone else working with you?"

"Just Steph and I, my daughter."

"Your daughter?" Ros stopped in her tracks.

Alex saw her expression and immediately explained. "My wife and I are divorced, just recently actually."

"Oh, I'm sorry. I didn't mean to pry."

"No, it's all right. It had been on the cards for a long time. She wanted something different from life. It's no big deal."

"These things are never easy, no matter how much sense they make at the time."

There was a recognition, a sudden understanding that each had known pain and disappointment. It didn't have to be talked about. It was in the past and both Alex and Ros were each looking to the future.

"Two questions." Alex said suddenly. What are you doing Saturday night? And do you like folk music?"

– Chapter 37 –

Ros had a spring in her step as she went into work on Friday morning. The upgrade was going well, new public-access computers were installed and she had managed, for the most part, to stay out of Karen's way. There was still an issue with her desk though. It seemed always to be in a state of disarray when she returned from her days off. She hadn't mentioned it, there were too many other things going on but she was becoming weary of having to constantly organise everything. She looked up to see Karen coming towards her. Maybe she could catch her off guard.

"Ah, Karen," she said, before Karen had the chance to say anything. "I'd like a word. Have you got a minute?"

Karen was clearly put out. "I was just coming to see you, Ros. What did you want to talk to me about? Let's get that out of the way first."

Ros ignored her comment. "It's about my desk, Karen. I don't know who's using it but I have to sort it out every time I come in. I never had this problem when Jennifer shared with me, so I know it's not her."

Karen raised her eyebrows. "And what, exactly, would you like me to do?"

"I would like you to tell me who, exactly, is using my desk so I can discuss the problem with him or her."

"Well, it's hardly 'your' desk really, is it?"

Ros didn't like where this was going but she had to know

what was happening. "What do you mean?"

"You may remember several weeks ago that I talked about changes in the pipeline."

Ros nodded and her brow furrowed.

"I'm looking at restructuring some sections and reassigning staff to allow them to use their unique skills."

Karen stopped talking, waiting for a reaction from Ros. She got none, other than a blank stare.

"The upshot is that I think you would be better placed in Reference. How do you feel about that?"

This was obviously Karen's attempt at consultation. Ros thought for a moment. She liked Reception but maybe working in a different section would offer the change she'd been looking for. Besides, a job was a job and it didn't really matter which section she worked in. "I don't know anything about working there but I don't mind changing."

"Don't worry, you'll get training. We'll have to change your contract, of course."

"Change my contract? Why?"

Karen raised her eyebrows again and pursed her lips. "Jennifer is now working in General Lending, full-time. Much of the new resources area will be next to Reference. We need you there full time, your contract will have to be changed."

Ros straightened her back.

"No."

"I beg your pardon?"

"I said, no. I can't work full time, I care for my mother. I don't mind job-sharing with someone."

"Not an option, I'm afraid."

"I see. Maybe I'll speak with someone from Human Resources." Ros got up to leave.

"I've spoken to the Board. Everyone is in favour of the new proposals."

"I'm not. You didn't speak to me. As I said, I don't mind sharing."

"No one to share with, we're understaffed."

"So who will be on Reception?"

"Grant."

"Grant? From the children's section? He's only been here, what, four months? How can he advise the public? He doesn't have enough experience of the library to be able to answer questions or offer suggestions. He can't even keep a desk tidy."

"He'll get the training he needs."

"So how are people 'using their unique skills' if they have to get training to do the job?"

Karen stared at her without speaking. Ros could see she was getting nowhere.

"So," Karen said after Ros had calmed down, "Could you report to Derek in Reference after your lunch break this afternoon, please? It's just for an informal, introductory chat. Thank you." Then she turned on her heels and walked off in the direction from which she had come, leaving Ros to her own thoughts, regardless of what they were.

Just before lunch, Ros got a message from her solicitor. Someone wanted to view her flat that evening. Ros would have to be there. This cheered her up and she began to put ideas together in her mind. They were vague, not fully formed, but the feeling she got was a curious mixture of excitement and apprehension. She was anxious about the changes at work but other aspects of her life seemed to be going well. A peculiar sense of calm washed over her and she couldn't help thinking she was being nudged in another direction.

Ros had to admit that her life had changed in so many ways in a very short space of time. She was living at her mum's for a start. Her mother was at home, where she wanted to be and carers were in place to help meet her needs. She was attending the day centre which she loved. She liked the staff and she was meeting people her own age and taking part in outings and activities. Ros had a bit more time to herself and Christmas was only weeks away. She had met Alex and that seemed to be going well. She had no intention of working full time. If things were changing so dramatically at work, she would find another job. That thought surprised her, but the clarity of it was undeniable. Perhaps she should start looking.

The viewing for her flat was at seven o'clock. Ros was early. The pictures that the solicitor had taken were very good but Ros knew that they could also give a false impression. She brought fresh flowers to put on the table and tried to anticipate questions that people might ask. She also planned to bring some more of her belongings back to her mother's house, so was able to take the time to decide what she wanted.

Ros felt nervous although she didn't know why. There seemed to be a lot of interest in the flat and if this person didn't buy it someone else would. Why was she so jittery? She checked the message again. It was a Mr Smith who was coming. Ros wondered if there would be a Mrs Smith as well.

The doorbell rang making her jump. She rushed to the door but tried to look calm as she opened it. She stared at the man in front of her.

"Hi Ros. Remember me?"

"Matthew?" Ros could hardly speak. She felt anger rising from somewhere in the depths but she didn't want a scene. She stood in the doorway, preventing him from coming in.

"What are you doing here?"

"I came to see you."

"Well, you've seen me. Good-bye." She went to close the door.

"Wait! We have to talk."

"We have nothing to talk about. Now, if you don't mind, I'm waiting for someone."

"Yes, Mr Smith, to view your flat. I'm Mr Smith. Aren't you going to show me round?"

Ros was astounded. "Deceitful as ever. Some things never change."

He ignored her words. "We have to talk."

"No, we don't." Ros went to close the door again but Matthew stepped forward.

"If you're selling the flat, I'm afraid we do."

She glared at him.

"Okay, if you won't let me come inside, we can talk on the doorstep. The point is, I lived here for eight years," Ros wondered where he was going with this. "And in that time I contributed to the upkeep of the property. Basically, what I'm saying is, I have a share in this flat and if you're going to sell it, I am entitled to a share of the profit."

It was some time before Ros spoke. "Matthew. I didn't know you had such a sense of humour. You're having a laugh." Her voice was getting louder and she had to work hard to restrain it. "Upkeep! You took more than you ever gave and you know it. You've got a nerve even coming here and you had to lie to do it. How are the gambling debts?"

Matthew looked to the floor.

"That's what I thought. Go!" She threw her left arm out to the side and pointed to the entrance at the front of the block. "Leave, now, and don't come back."

"I was hoping we could sort this out between us, Ros. Save all the faff of making a legal claim."

"A legal claim? Where do you get these stupid ideas? There is nothing to sort out." She was almost yelling again. She took a deep breath. "Well, I don't know about you, but I have better things to do." She tried to close the door again.

"I'm not going to give up on this, Ros. When you think about it, you know I'm right."

"Are you? Tell you what, then. You get your solicitor to write to my solicitor with your 'legal claim' and we'll see how far that gets you."

"That's not a bad idea," Matthew said, cocking his head to one side. "I had hoped to settle this amicably but have it your way. See you in court, Honey."

Ros slammed the door. Rage filled her whole being. 'The arrogance of the man! She shouted. "The bare-faced cheek, turning up here like that."

It was some time before she felt calm enough to go back to her mother's. She had thought of throwing the flowers in the bin but she didn't want to let Matthew make her feel that way. Deciding they were too nice to waste she wrapped them up to take home for her mum. She would phone her solicitor in the morning to see what her legal position was, just in case.

– Chapter 38 –

It had been a long time since Ros went out on a date. She felt a little self-conscious and wondered if she had made the right decision in accepting. She liked Alex but he had just come through a divorce and Ros couldn't help wondering why he had asked her out. She didn't want to be caught on the rebound. What if his wife was still on the scene? What if he was using her as some kind of therapy for a broken heart? Of course, he could actually like her.

She sighed. If she had learned anything it was that there were no guarantees in life and, it felt good to be going out again, socialising. She might even enjoy herself. Besides, what else would she be doing on a Saturday night?

She brushed her hair and tried to put it up the way she used to but it was too short. She sighed and pinned it back at the sides with some pretty hair clips. She wasn't sure where Alex was taking her, but dinner and a pub had been mentioned. She had worried about leaving her mum on her own but when she said she'd been asked out on a date, her mum said it was about time and mentioned something about lipstick. That pang of guilt was back but her mother had insisted she go and Ros knew the carers would be in to help her mum.

"You have given up enough of your time on me," she had said. "You do so much for everyone else but not yourself. Go out, have fun. You've got a key in case I'm in bed when you get home." Her mother had smiled and given her a little wink. Ros had no argument to give her.

Despite her concerns, Ros was looking forward to the evening. Alex was attractive, certainly, but there was more than that. She had felt a strange kind of connection the first time she had seen him. She hadn't even known who he was, just a man in a waiting room, and she began to wonder what it was that drew people together.

She was thinking too much. It was only a date and it would give them both a chance to get to know each other. Who knows? They could be great friends.

– or more

The thought surprised her, and worried her a little. She hadn't been out with another man in such a long time, she worried now that she had forgotten how to act, how to make conversation. She counted back. It was ten years since she had even been open to the thought of a relationship.

But why was she thinking about a relationship anyway? This was only a date. Depending on how things went tonight, there might not be another one. Somehow that didn't feel right so she dismissed the idea. She looked at herself in the mirror and smiled. She was slim, petite and still quite shapely. 'Not bad, for a middle-aged woman,' she thought. But there was one more thing to do. She put on the green dress and that made all the difference. She was ready.

When her mother saw her she gasped. "You look wonderful," she beamed. "Absolutely wonderful."

"Oh, thank you Mum. I feel good too. I won't be late back, don't worry."

"I'm not worried, Darling. You have a good time."

Ros heard the doorbell. Alex was early.

The Italian restaurant was beautiful. It was in a little side street just off the main road in town and Ros had never seen it before. Although they were inside, the decor was akin to a street cafe and, despite it being a cold, winter evening, she could almost believe that she was sitting at a little table in some piazza with the bright, Mediterranean sun warming her whole body. The food, the wine and the conversation were most agreeable and Ros found herself relaxing in the company of this man she had only seen for the first time a little over a month ago.

"What made you open a book shop?" she asked.

"It's just something I've always wanted to do. I never had the chance before. When Charlotte and I divorced six months ago, the house was sold and everything split fifty-fifty. I put some of my money into the business."

Ros realised she didn't even know where he lived but thought now might not be the best time to ask. Alex saved her the trouble.

"I rent a flat not far from where Dad lives. It's good to be close to him. When I saw the shop for sale, something clicked and I just knew I had to get it."

Ros knew exactly what he meant. "It's good to pay attention to these little nudges," she offered. "Steph seems a lovely girl."

"Oh, she's a gem. She's still living with her mum but she's off to university in Edinburgh next September. I don't know what I'm going to do without her. She's the creative one. She does all the displays."

"She's very good at it. What's she studying?"

"Art."

"Perfect. She'll come back with loads of ideas."

"I hope so. I'll miss her though."

"September's a long way off."

"It will go quickly, I know it will. In fact, she might even leave before that. There's talk of her friends sharing a flat so she might be away by summer."

"Edinburgh's not that far. It will be easy for her to visit."

"That's true. And I can always send her a message if I'm not sure what to do with this or that. She's so well organised, quite the businesswoman. Anyway, tell me about you."

Ros talked about her job and all the changes that were going on. He knew about her mum having been in hospital and how desperate she was to get home again, but he hadn't known about some of the hurdles Ros had to jump to make that happen. She even mentioned putting her flat on the market so she could stay with her mum permanently. Conversation flowed easily between them.

"Fancy a nightcap?" Alex asked when they had finished their meal.

"I don't want to be out too late."

"It's early, yet. Just one? I know this little pub, not far from home."

Ros agreed.

The taxi followed the familiar roads that Ros drove every working day. It dropped them off on a busy street about three-quarters along her usual route. Ros looked around but could see no sign of a pub. After walking along the road a short distance, she could hear music and a moment later they turned a corner and she saw the pub in front of them.

It was busy inside and they were lucky to find a table along the back wall. Ros wasn't familiar with folk music but found it lively and fun and she tapped along with its beat. Alex got up when the band had finished their set. He talked with the lead singer then brought him over to the table and introduced Ros to him. It seemed like Alex and Bill had known each other for some time and they talked and laughed easily together. Ros began to wonder if Alex had some musical ability.

By the end of the evening, Ros was feeling a little giddy despite having had very little to drink. If it had been a warm, summer evening, they might have walked home, but it was cold and the rain was coming on. The taxi took only minutes to get Ros home. Alex walked to the door with her.

"I had a brilliant evening, Alex. My head is still reeling from the music, and the company."

"Yeah, it wasn't bad was it?"

"Not bad at all," Ros agreed.

They stood in silence for a moment, then Alex stepped forward and gently kissed her cheek.

"We should do it again."

– Chapter 39 –

Monday morning came and Ros was anxious to phone her solicitor first thing, however work seemed to be busier than usual. People were coming and going in all directions. She got on with her duties, deciding it would be better to phone during her break. At least that way, she would have some privacy. Why couldn't her solicitor have been open on Saturday like her mum's was? This could all have been dealt with. She took a deep breath. There was no point in getting stressed about it; Saturday or today, it didn't matter.

By mid-morning, she had dealt with numerous queries from members of staff as well as the public. Her mouth was dry and she wanted to escape to the staff room. Once there, she immediately reached for her phone, called her solicitor and relayed the events from Friday evening in as much detail as she could remember. She tried to keep her anger at bay but it must have shown through, at least a little. Mr Chambers was sympathetic. He listened carefully, considering everything she told him.

"I really don't think you have anything to worry about, Miss Malcolm. This gentleman..."

"Huh! He's no gentleman." The words were out of her mouth before she could stop them and she felt the blood rise to her cheeks. She was glad they were on the phone rather than talking face to face. "Forgive me, Mr Chambers. I didn't mean to be abrupt."

"That's no problem, Miss Malcolm. His name is Matthew?"

"Yes," Ros said meekly.

"Well, Matthew would have to present documentation to substantiate his claim. Do you think he can do that?"

"What kind of documentation?"

"Bank statements, receipts, something that proves he paid for things with his own money. You say you didn't have a joint account?"

Ros confirmed that they had kept separate accounts and that she had paid the mortgage, utility bills, decoration and maintenance on the property, confirming that she had the required paperwork to prove it. The only thing Matthew had contributed to had been grocery shopping, most of which he had eaten. She thought of the things that had gone missing from the flat, mostly ornaments and small household items but some pieces of jewellery as well. At the time she thought she had just misplaced them but they had never been found. When she discovered his debts, she had challenged him. Not only had he denied taking anything, he had also accused her of being forgetful of where she put things and trying to blame it on him. It had led to a huge row, each accusing the other of whatever came to mind, and had ended with Ros yelling at him to get out and Matthew slamming the door as he left.

For a while, she thought that perhaps she had been to blame. Maybe she had misplaced things; maybe they could have worked it out together. But after some time she dismissed these notions knowing the situation would never have changed, Matthew would never have changed, and that splitting up was the right thing to do.

Of course, she had no proof that he had stolen and sold any of her property, so she said nothing to Mr Chambers. She simply explained the circumstances around the breakup by citing Matthew's gambling as the main reason, adding that she had lent him money which had never been repaid.

After some discussion, Mr Chambers had put Ros' mind at ease, stating that, if he were to receive a letter from Matthew's solicitor, he had all the information he needed for a speedy and determined response. Ros breathed a sigh of relief and thanked him.

Mr Chambers had given Ros an update on her flat, saying that there was a great deal of interest and that he felt she would have no trouble getting her asking price, possibly more. Ros found this very encouraging. If that was the case, she could pay off her mortgage and still have a considerable sum of money in the bank. An idea began to form in her mind. Now that her costs were greatly reduced, she could afford to take a little break from working, perhaps the whole winter. This idea grew the more she thought about it. On the way back to her desk, she stopped to see Sam in Human Resources.

"Enjoy your break, Ros?"

Ros didn't know how long Karen had been waiting but, by the look on her face, it may have been some time.

"Yes I did Karen. I really did. Thank you for asking."

Karen looked unsettled. "Sorry I didn't get a chance to speak to you on Friday. Did you manage to have a chat with Derek?"

"Derek is such a lovely person and would be a joy to work with."

"Excellent," she said. There was uncertainty in her voice. Ros was being nice. She was losing ground and she knew it. "I've asked Grant to come and see you this afternoon. You can show him what's involved here."

"Absolutely no problem, Karen."

Tiny beads of sweat began to appear on Karen's forehead. Something was wrong. She wasn't in control and didn't know how to deal with it. She rallied herself.

"So, I take it from your acceptance that you're happy to train Grant for Reception duties and happy to work full-time in Reference?"

"I would be delighted to train Grant for Reception duties but I will not be working in Reference."

Karen was floored. "I don't understand."

"I'm resigning, Karen."

"You can't do that!"

"Yes, I can, and I did. I've told Sam already and will have it in writing tomorrow morning. I know I have to give a month's notice but I still have a few weeks leave to take so, I suppose, effectively, I could finish at the end of next week. I'll see what HR say and let you know."

Ros had never seen Karen speechless before. The smirk that usually covered her face was gone and she stood, mouth gaping, trying to take in what was happening. Ros almost felt sorry for her.

"Don't worry. I'll teach Grant all I can this week. He should pick it up quickly. After all, he has his unique skills to help him. He could come over now, if he's free. I can start by showing him how to keep a desk tidy."

By the time evening came, Ros was beginning to wonder if she had done the right thing in resigning. Although she would have money in the bank, she wouldn't have an income and her nest-egg wouldn't last forever. Yet it felt right and she had learned to trust her feelings. Her job was becoming tedious and it would be easy enough to get a part-time job at a later date. She could give herself a break from work to be with her mum;

take up a hobby; maybe even think about a course at college; all the things she'd been thinking about. She liked this new-found freedom.

It occurred to Ros that she hadn't seen Suzanne for some time. How could she have missed her? They usually saw each other when she came in to work in the Archives. Perhaps she should give her a call. Although the intention was there, it seemed that something always happened to confound her.

Christmas came and went. Ros and her mother invited Mr Fielding and Alex for Christmas dinner. It was good to have company in the house. Ros did the cooking, her mother did the socialising.

Ros sent Suzanne a card and received one from her as well. She had put a little note in Suzanne's card saying sorry they had missed each other and suggesting they meet up some time after the holidays. Suzanne had said something similar in her card but, so far neither had replied. Most of Ros' time was spent with either her mother or with Alex. She was as comfortable with him as he seemed to be with her. They liked the same foods, the same films, the same music. In fact, there was little that they disagreed on.

The New Year had made her think about priorities. She realised that home, family and friends were important but so was taking some time for herself. She didn't make resolutions anymore. Usually they had been abandoned by February. She thought about all that had happened in recent months. There had been the conflict and upheaval that she'd had to face, both at work and at home, but she had overcome it. There had been help too, she didn't have to face it all alone. She thought of her dreams, the message James had given her, and Suzanne who had always been there for her when she needed help. Ros had learned to ask for help when she needed it and to offer it when it was required. She had learned to give and to receive, and know the balance between the two. She picked up the phone and gave her friend a call. Ros had to leave a message on Suzanne's home phone and, after three days, had not received a reply. There was no hurry. She knew Suzanne would have been busy with her family over the holidays and would get back to her when she could.

– Chapter 40 –

The holidays were over and things were beginning to fall back into their normal routine. Everything seemed to slow down, now that Ros wasn't working. When her mum was offered a second place at the Day Centre, she accepted it without hesitation and this meant that Ros now had Wednesdays and Fridays to herself.

Ros looked out the window. The weather was wet and miserable. 'Dreich' was an apt Scottish word for it; not only for the weather itself but for how a person felt about it. Her mother's Day Centre activities had started up again and Ros had to hold the umbrella over her mum's head while she helped her onto the minibus that first morning. She raced back to the kitchen to put the kettle on again as soon as the bus had gone. Sipping her tea, she began to consider her options. She opened her laptop and found short courses both at the college and some that were held at local community centres. There was a lot to choose from, even a course on baking bread. That would be interesting as well as practical. Unable to make up her mind, she decided to wait, give herself time to settle down and do nothing for a while. She was enjoying this slower pace. There was no rush, she could look again later.

She felt drawn to The Book Keeper, not only because it was Alex's shop but also because she enjoyed being there. It had an atmosphere that was welcoming and friendly. If it wasn't busy, she could sit by the fireplace with its electric, log-effect fire, drinking coffee and reading a book. She could spend all day there. Reading for enjoyment had been a distant concept for such a long time, but now it was slowly becoming part of her routine again and her home library was growing.

Ros began helping out at the book shop. It had been Steph's suggestion.

"I'm not really that keen on books," she had confided to Ros one day when she came in for a hot chocolate. Alex was upstairs checking a delivery and the girls had a chance to talk.

"Really?" This was not something Ros had expected to hear. "So you're just helping your dad out."

"I'm happy to do what I can, but this is his project. He's really keen and I hope it works out well for him. He's a hard worker. I just don't share his enthusiasm. Don't get me wrong. I like books, all right."

"You'd have to if you're going to university, I would imagine."

"But that's for art. That's different."

"I see."

"I mean, I like working here and everything, but Dad's the one who knows about the books, the authors, the storylines, all of that. I don't. So if customers ask questions, I have to get Dad to talk to them."

"Your dad says you do the displays."

"Yeah. I love doing that."

"You're very good at it."

"Ahh, thanks Ros." Steph seemed genuinely taken with the compliment. "The thing is, and I hope you don't mind me saying this, but you and Dad seem to get on really well together and, well, I think he would like to have you here. It would give me more time to see my friends before I go away."

"And I suppose it would help you relax and focus on your studies if you knew your dad had someone here with him."

"Yeah, there's a bit of that too."

They both laughed.

Ros liked the idea and spoke to Alex about it. Alex loved the idea and they agreed on one day a week, at least to start with. Fridays were often busy and that suited Ros. She could see her mum onto the minibus and be back in time for her coming home. It was perfect.

Ros knew this was an informal arrangement. Her 'payment' would be all the coffee or hot chocolate she could drink. She was happy with that.

– Chapter 41 –

When Ros checked her phone, she found she had missed a call from Suzanne. She phoned back but the call went straight to voicemail. Not wanting to leave a long message, she simply said that she was sorry to have missed the call and hoped they could meet up soon. It was later that evening when Suzanne phoned again.

"It's so good to talk to you," Suzanne said. "We have loads to catch up on."

"I know. So much has happened lately. When are you free?"

"I can only do Wednesday or Thursday next week, unless you want to leave it for a while."

"No. I've got way too much to tell you. Wednesday would be best."

"Okay, where do you want to meet?

"I know this lovely little place. They do the best coffee in town."

"I like the sound of that." Suzanne laughed.

Ros gave Suzanne directions of where they could meet without actually telling her what the name of the shop was. She wanted to keep that a surprise.

When Wednesday came, they met at the local supermarket and walked the short distance along the street to their destination.

When they stopped, Suzanne looked up, intrigued. "A book shop?"

Ros nodded and walked forward to open the door but turned

suddenly, looked at Suzanne and said, "By the way, I've met someone."

Suzanne's eyes widened. "'*Bye the way*'? You don't say 'by the way' for something like that."

Ros beamed. "I'd like you to meet him." She pushed the door all the way open and walked in. Suzanne followed, not really sure what to expect. As they entered the book shop Alex looked up and his smile filled the room. Ros introduced Suzanne who was clearly delighted for her friend.

Alex was charming. He asked what they would like and said he would bring it over to the table. They ordered coffee – cappuccino for Suzanne and latte for Ros – along with a slice of lemon cake each and sat at the little table by the window. Ros wanted to catch up with Suzanne, find out what was happening with her and her family. She realised that she knew very little about her. They always seemed to be talking about Ros all the time and discussing what was going on in her life. A wave of regret washed over her. Now was the time to change that. But first she had to tell Suzanne all about how she met Alex. When she looked, Suzanne had tears in her eyes.

"Are you all right?"

"Yes, I'm fine," Suzanne said, getting a tissue from her bag. "I'm just so happy for you."

Ros touched her friend's arm reassuringly.

Suzanne put the tissue away, took a sip of her coffee and said, "Right. Tell me everything."

Ros told her how she had first seen him in the hospital waiting area of the ward her mum was in but, apart from thinking he was attractive, hadn't thought any more about it. She went on to give details of how events had unfolded to bring them both to where they are now.

“Isn’t it funny, when you think about it, how everything has to be in exactly the right place at exactly the right time for these things to happen?”

“I suppose so.” Ros’ said. “I’d never really thought about it like that before.”

Suzanne had mentioned the word ‘synchronicity’. Ros made a mental note to look it up when she got home.

“Sounds like you’ve been busy,” Suzanne was saying.

“Busy enough,” Ros replied. “Mum and I discussed my staying with her permanently so, I’ve also put my flat on the market.”

Suzanne’s eyebrows raised. “You’re selling your flat?”

“Yes, and you’ll never guess...”

Suzanne drew closer, urging her on. “What?”

“Matthew turned up at the flat.”

“What! After all this time? Why?”

“He seemed to think I owed him something; claimed he was entitled to a share of the profit from the sale.”

“I don’t believe it!” Suzanne exclaimed and sat back in her chair.

“Honestly.” Ros said. “I’m listening to myself telling you and I can hardly believe it either.”

They discussed this situation at length, including Ros contacting her solicitor. Suzanne was astounded. There was a lot more to tell and Suzanne asked a million questions. Ros ordered another coffee for each of them. When she mentioned leaving her job, Suzanne was speechless.

“It just seemed the right thing to do,” Ros said.

Suzanne nodded. “I know you’ve been unhappy there for some time.”

“Yes, I was. And with all the changes that were being imposed,

I thought the time was right. I believe others have left since then as well."

Ros knew Suzanne would want to know these things but she was aware that they were talking about her again. She wanted to know about her friend too.

"Anyway, what about you? Did you enjoy the holidays?"

"Oh, I've been busy too," Suzanne said. "You might remember I told you my husband was due to retire this year?"

"Yes, I remember that."

"Well, it wasn't supposed to be till the end of this year but he got the opportunity to go early. It makes little difference financially so we decided that we would do that and use the money to do a bit of travelling. We're thinking about buying a caravan."

"A caravan?"

"Yes, I'm not that keen, really. We're pensioners now and I like my comfort. I'm thinking more about hotels or guesthouses but Frank likes camping and it would be better than a tent."

"So it's a compromise."

"Yes, but it's still under discussion." Suzanne laughed. "Anyway, we're planning to see more of Scotland. It's such a beautiful country and I don't like flying anyway. We hope to be away a lot so don't worry if you don't hear from me for a while. There are lots of places that don't get a good phone signal."

Alex came over and joined them. Conversation was easy and Suzanne watched the interaction between Ros and him. She smiled, knowing they would both be happy together. Before leaving, Ros showed Suzanne the upstairs. She loved the cosy space and the fireplace in particular. They both took some time to browse and both ended up buying some books. Ros got one on anatomy and physiology, thinking of her long, lost nursing career. Maybe she could learn a therapy. If nothing else, it would enhance her First Aid skills. She also bought a book on knitting and crochet for her mum. Not that she needed another knitting book, but Ros liked the look of it. Suzanne only bought one, *A Campers Guide to Scotland*. She was tempted to get more but decided space might be limited in a caravan.

– Chapter 42 –

When they got outside the two friends looked at each other and neither spoke for a moment. It was Suzanne who broke the silence.

"I'm so glad we met up, Ros. It was good to have had this time to spend together."

Ros had a strange feeling, almost as if Suzanne was saying good-bye forever. A tinge of sadness caught her unawares and her body tensed. Was this a parting of the ways? She didn't want to lose her friend but accepted that they each had their own journey. Ros found comfort in the thought that they could still phone each other, still meet for coffee from time to time. True friendship is never lost. She felt the muscles in her back soften. She smiled and gave Suzanne a warm and affectionate hug.

"You've been such a good friend to me, Suzanne. Thank you so much for all your help and support. I mean it. I don't know what I would have done without you."

"It works both ways, Ros. You've been there for me when I needed you as well."

"We can still meet up sometimes, can't we?"

"Absolutely."

There was more silence.

"Well, I guess I better go," Ros sighed. "I've got to pick up some shopping and get home in time for Mum getting back.

"Yes, I better go too," Suzanne replied. "I want to have a quick look through this book before Frank comes in." She held the book propped against her forearm looking at it as if it was a tablet of stone. She touched the cover as she spoke. "I wonder if I can talk him into going out for dinner," she said looking up. "I don't feel like cooking tonight."

Suzanne had parked further down by the flats and had to head in the opposite direction to Ros. They said good-bye again and promised, again, to keep in touch.

Suzanne stood for a while in the High Street watching Ros as she headed towards the supermarket. She knew her friend didn't need her any more. She knew the dream had done its work and Ros was where she needed to be to get on with her life. The street was getting busy as shoppers hurried home before the children got out of school. Suzanne stepped aside to let them pass. She found a convenient bench in front of the railings of a small car park, and sat down. People hurried by, taking no notice of her.

Looking up towards the sky she said, "I think she'll be fine. I know she'll be fine. She's finally content and happy with her life. She couldn't have continued as things were. She has a future and she can finally see her way forward. It was all I could have wished for her. The situation with her mum is working out quite well, don't you think?"

She paused, as if listening.

"Yes, I know her mum will have to leave her, but not for some time yet, not till she's ready. Ros will mourn her, of course, but it's the nature of things here. Don't people have some interesting ways of expressing that? They use phrases like 'pass away', 'shuttle off this mortal coil', or just the word 'die', like it's final. My favourite is 'pop their clogs'. That's hilarious, but then, they often use humour to deal with things that frighten them. It's all the same thing, and they make such a fuss about it. Her mum will be fine, of course, but Ros won't know that, although, I think she might sense it. She's really opening up."

She paused again.

"I was a bit concerned about that. I knew she had to leave her job and I'd hoped the soft approach would work. It nearly did but she needed that extra nudge."

Another pause.

"Well, she handled it very well. It might have seemed drastic, pitting her against someone so confrontational, but that challenge was needed to take her out of her comfort zone. I think she showed great courage, and confidence. She had to have the space to move forward. Sometimes you have to let go of the old to make room for the new. That was one of the lessons she had to learn.

"She dealt with the other scenarios in the same way, like Matthew turning up 'out of the blue' like that. Was that you're idea?" Suzanne furrowed her brow and raised her eyes to the clouds, giving her a slightly stern expression. "And that Charge Nurse!" she continued. "Ros kept cool and put her case forward in a calm and rational way. And look how successful that was. I'm proud of her. I know I'm not supposed to be proud, but I am. Okay? And she did it all herself. I just helped to guide her, gave her little nudges here and there. Actually, I thought James was going to blow my cover when we went to that meeting in the library. I knew he could see me, see my energy.

"I'm glad we decided to use the dream to reawaken those traits that were dormant. That worked well. She's quite perceptive, really. Everything had to be in place before she met Alex. I know Alex was always on the cards for Ros, but she had to be ready. He's a fine man, an honest and sincere man. Ros had to regain her trust in people, men in particular. At last she is open to new possibilities, new adventures."

Suzanne straightened her back, then stood and headed in the direction of where her car was parked. Looking up to the sky as she walked, she said, "Job done. All is as it should be. She's going to be fine."

She stood for a moment, listening again, then bowing her head, said "Thank you" before stepping forward and disappearing into the crowd.

Acknowledgements

My constant friends Carolann Erskine and Jackie Hay for their love, feedback and amazing proofreading skills;

My writing buddies at City Writers and the Novel Writing Group for reading my work and giving me honest and helpful feedback;

Ashley Campbell for her enthusiasm in producing such beautiful artwork for the cover;

Shirley Brennan, friend and fellow therapist, for her help with the dream sequence and the intricacies of energy flow;

My beautiful family for keeping me going during the sticky times and helping with my website and social media queries;

And my wonderful husband, Neil for being there with love, support and cups of tea, lots of tea.